THE TWAIN DOES MEET

A Jolie and Scoobie Novella

ELAINE L. ORR

Copyright © 2019 Elaine L. Orr

All rights reserved.

Library of Congress Control Number:
ISBN: 978-1-948070-41-6

DEDICATION

To blended families everywhere

ACKNOWLEDGMENTS

Thanks to the Decatur, Illinois "Write Stuff" Critique Group, whose members are generous with their time and comments. And to my sister, Diane Orr-Fisher, for her always spot-on comments and eagle eye.

CHAPTER ONE

IN THE FOUR MONTHS SINCE Scoobie and I were joined by his much-younger brother on New Year's Eve, the three of us and our pets have worked hard to get along. We usually do, though sometimes it's challenging.

Aunt Madge sat us down and said big changes could be really good and really hard at the same time. She said we would sometimes "hit glitches," as she called them, "and need to talk them out."

She wasn't just basking on the sand.

I sat on the couch with my feet on the coffee table, and thought about how well Scoobie and Terry had bonded since Terry arrived in Ocean Alley. Their senses of humor were wackier than mine, and I didn't mind saying they each probably had twenty IQ points on me.

And they wouldn't let me share their grief.

Terry had been very close to their dad, who was in his mid-fifties when his younger son was born. Terence's second wife sounded like a wonderful woman, and they had doted on their young son. After her early death from cancer, he focused on keeping Terry happy and well adjusted.

Scoobie had barely known the man who left when he was twelve, and many of Scoobie's memories included his ill-tempered mother shouting at Terence about his drinking. Scoobie had spoken little about his father before the man showed up in town with then ten-year-old Terry – and died before Scoobie had a chance to talk to him.

After our first few weeks living in the crowded two-bedroom Ocean Alley bungalow, the brothers had come to understand each other completely, and Scoobie had the chance to learn about their father's better qualities. He decided that Terry didn't need to hear about too many of his bad memories. I wished I had been privy to more about the brothers' conversations.

Sometimes I wonder if Terry feels awkward because my last name is different than his and Scoobie's, which is O'Brien. I like my name – Jolie Gentil – though I'm glad few people know it means 'pretty nice' in French. Eventually he figured out that

Aunt Madge had kept her last name – Richards – when she married Harry Steele. That seemed to eliminate some of his uncertainty.

It's hard to be eleven.

Oh well. I have more to focus on than Terry's adjustment to us and Ocean Alley. I am seven months pregnant. Preceded by the beach ball that is my tummy, I continue to work as a real estate appraiser, manage the Harvest for All Food Pantry, and serve as chief meal planner and grocery shopper. And I almost always want to nap.

Jazz meowed from her spot on the end table on the other side of the couch. My black cat and I arrived in Ocean Alley together when I came to Aunt Madge's B&B at the end of my first marriage, almost four years ago. Scoobie is the most important touchstone in my life now, but Jazz remains a close second.

I pointed an index finger at the cat. She used to perch on the back of the couch, on a cloth placemat, but seems to have decided that I moved around too much right now. After I threw her off the table a couple of times I finally moved the place mat to the end table, and it has become her napping spot. I pick my battles.

"You have food in your bowl."

Jazz stared at me, and I realized she wanted me to know that Pebbles was en route from her spot under Terry's bed. I hadn't noticed the clicking of our pet skunk's nails on the hardwood floor.

Pebbles entered the living room, gave me an inscrutable look, and turned toward the kitchen. Her bowl of Skunkie Delights sits next to Jazz's bowl and, more important, her litter box is in the closet by the back door.

I sighed and heaved myself off the couch. I wanted to be sure that closet door was ajar.

Jazz hopped on the floor and darted ahead of Pebbles. Ever since I'd acquired the pet skunk, which had belonged to the deceased, prior owner of our bungalow, my black cat made sure she asserted her role as 'first pet.'

"Listen you two, I have more important things to do than cater to your needs."

I finished filling food and water bowls and resettled myself on the couch. I had just gone back to making a list of food pantry chores and home appraisal appointments when footsteps pounded on the sidewalk leading to the house. Terry almost fell through the front door. From the frown on his face when he walked into the living room, today appeared to be a glitch day.

I stopped mid-greeting. "What is it?"

He tossed his brown hair from his forehead – he'd needed it cut for weeks but kept evading the issue. "My jerk locker mate told me to mind my own business when I asked him if he was okay."

I frowned. I'd only met Eddie briefly, at a back-to-school night. "You guys usually get along. Is he sick or something?"

Terry stooped to pet Jazz who wound herself between his legs. "Like I care."

I hesitated before saying, "You must care a little, or you wouldn't be upset."

He plopped in the rocking chair across from the sofa. "He said it when a bunch of other people were near our locker."

"Ah." Sounded as if Terry had been embarrassed. "He shouldn't have said that."

"He's been crabby all week." Terry stood. "I'm making a PB&J and going to Kevin's. You want some milk or something?"

"Too healthy." I grinned. "I made some powdered chocolate milk a few minutes ago."

Terry went into his bedroom, which also serves as Scoobie's reading area, and I heard him rummage in his closet for his soccer ball and shin guards. Then he headed to the kitchen.

I glanced at the cube-shaped clock radio on a table next to the rocking chair. Three-fifteen. Scoobie would be home no later than three-thirty. He used to be home by now. I think he's giving Terry and me alone time after school. I haven't let him know I've caught on.

Terry returned to the couch with his PB&J and some potato chips rolled into a paper towel. Jazz trotted behind him. He grinned. "I gave her two treats."

"You're her new best friend."

"I have been for a while."

I pointed at Jazz. "You're so ornery." I patted the cushion next to me, and Jazz jumped up to sit by Terry on the rocker.

Terry smirked, but didn't laugh. He took a huge bite of his PB&J. "So, Jolie. You think I should talk to Eddie tomorrow?"

"It seems..." A car door slammed in the driveway and Terry bounded off the chair, Jazz following.

"Traitor," I muttered. Almost on cue, Pebbles, waddled back into the room. Maybe she was trying to tell me she'd always be my loyal buddy. *Oh, joy.*

Terry opened the screen door and Scoobie cuffed him on the shoulder as he walked in. "Gotta say, Terry, I hope your day was better than mine."

Pebbles turned back toward Terry's bedroom. She likes Scoobie, but she isn't big on crowds.

Terry didn't miss a beat. "We can have a contest later. What's up?"

Scoobie tossed his lightweight jacket on the arm of the rocker and bent over me. "How's my favorite Preggo?"

I leaned toward him and we kissed lightly. "She's good. We want to hear about your day." And I certainly did. Scoobie rarely says he's had a bad day.

I frowned. I'd only met Eddie briefly, at a back-to-school night. "You guys usually get along. Is he sick or something?"

Terry stooped to pet Jazz who wound herself between his legs. "Like I care."

I hesitated before saying, "You must care a little, or you wouldn't be upset."

He plopped in the rocking chair across from the sofa. "He said it when a bunch of other people were near our locker."

"Ah." Sounded as if Terry had been embarrassed. "He shouldn't have said that."

"He's been crabby all week." Terry stood. "I'm making a PB&J and going to Kevin's. You want some milk or something?"

"Too healthy." I grinned. "I made some powdered chocolate milk a few minutes ago."

Terry went into his bedroom, which also serves as Scoobie's reading area, and I heard him rummage in his closet for his soccer ball and shin guards. Then he headed to the kitchen.

I glanced at the cube-shaped clock radio on a table next to the rocking chair. Three-fifteen. Scoobie would be home no later than three-thirty. He used to be home by now. I think he's giving Terry and me alone time after school. I haven't let him know I've caught on.

Terry returned to the couch with his PB&J and some potato chips rolled into a paper towel. Jazz trotted behind him. He grinned. "I gave her two treats."

"You're her new best friend."

"I have been for a while."

I pointed at Jazz. "You're so ornery." I patted the cushion next to me, and Jazz jumped up to sit by Terry on the rocker.

Terry smirked, but didn't laugh. He took a huge bite of his PB&J. "So, Jolie. You think I should talk to Eddie tomorrow?"

"It seems..." A car door slammed in the driveway and Terry bounded off the chair, Jazz following.

"Traitor," I muttered. Almost on cue, Pebbles, waddled back into the room. Maybe she was trying to tell me she'd always be my loyal buddy. *Oh, joy.*

Terry opened the screen door and Scoobie cuffed him on the shoulder as he walked in. "Gotta say, Terry, I hope your day was better than mine."

Pebbles turned back toward Terry's bedroom. She likes Scoobie, but she isn't big on crowds.

Terry didn't miss a beat. "We can have a contest later. What's up?"

Scoobie tossed his lightweight jacket on the arm of the rocker and bent over me. "How's my favorite Preggo?"

I leaned toward him and we kissed lightly. "She's good. We want to hear about your day." And I certainly did. Scoobie rarely says he's had a bad day.

He took one of Terry's potato chips. "Hits the spot." He sat next to me on the couch and Terry sat across from us in the rocker.

Scoobie rolled his shoulders. "I let myself get stressed. Sam told us at a staff meeting that they might have to cut one position from the Radiology Department. He said he was giving us a heads up so we could work at the top of our game. Maybe the hospital management would change their minds or take a job from somewhere else."

Sometimes Scoobie's boss, Sam, is a pain in the tailbone, but he's always above board. If he thought someone might lose their job, he'd give fair warning.

Terry spoke in almost a whisper. "Could it be you?"

Scoobie seemed to sense that something bugged Terry besides Scoobie's job situation. "What's up, Terry? I don't think it would be me, but there are other jobs for x-ray techs in the area."

Terry's brow smoothed. "They'd be nuts to get rid of you."

Scoobie grinned, which emphasized how much alike the two brothers looked. Scoobie was blonde with a beard, and Terry had brown hair – and no beard at age eleven. But it was more than appearance. They had the same irreverent humor and even walked at a similar fast clip.

"I mean," Scoobie said, "they'd be crazy to get rid of the best-looking guy in the department."

"And the most modest," I said, dryly.

Terry smiled. "I won't worry. About that."

Scoobie frowned. "About what, then?"

Terry told his tale of Eddie's insult, said within hearing distance of other kids. Compared to the prospect of layoffs at the hospital it wasn't that big a deal. But Terry was eleven, and nothing mattered more than friends. Or at least their opinions.

Scoobie listened intently. "You don't know what else is bugging him?"

Terry shrugged. "I think his dad gets on his case sometimes, but he didn't talk about anything different."

Scoobie nodded. "He shouldn't be rude, but maybe tomorrow you can ask him what's up."

Terry shrugged. "I guess. Or maybe I won't use the locker much the next couple of days."

"Ignoring doesn't make it go away," Scoobie said.

I met Terry's gaze. "I've been known to try that."

Scoobie snorted. "We won't tell him how well that's worked for you sometimes."

Terry's eyebrows went up. "You can tell me."

"Later," I said. "Weren't you going to find Kevin for some soccer practice?"

When he had left, Scoobie slid closer to me and rubbed my shoulders. "And you thought we wouldn't deal with stuff like this for another decade."

"Early practice, I suppose." I kissed the hand he had on my right shoulder. "He's so good about everything. I hate to see him hurting even a little."

Scoobie squeezed my shoulder. "He'll figure it out. We have to let him."

"I suppose. And I need to focus on Harvest for All."

Scoobie looked puzzled for a second. "Oh, right, the meeting tonight."

I nodded. I needed to switch gears. "I made a meatloaf earlier. I figured we could eat fast and then head over to the church for the Harvest for All meeting." I hoped this would be my last meeting as chair for a while. It was probably wishful thinking to imagine someone would take over the food pantry job permanently.

"Ah yes," Scoobie said. "More fun stuff to figure out."

WHEN REVEREND JAMISON talked me into assuming leadership for the Harvest for All Food Pantry, I figured I'd do it for a short time and find someone else to take over – someone more dedicated to the work. And better at herding cats. That's how I thought of our diverse group of volunteers.

We drove to First Presbyterian, in the heart of downtown Ocean Alley's business district, an elaborate term for a couple square blocks that contain the courthouse, city hall, and a few stores. As we got out of the car, I thought again that the church's traditional red brick and white trim didn't hint at the busy food pantry in its basement.

Scoobie and I got to the meeting room, just down the hall from the pantry itself, a few minutes before the others. My hope was that Megan, my favorite volunteer, would agree to chair for at least a few months. But she now ran the Java Jolt Coffee Shop, so she might not have time.

That would leave few options. Dr. George Welby often speaks at boom level, though he tones it down once a meeting starts. However, he's made it clear he's getting up there, as he says, and can't do as much. The mild-mannered Monica often wears a cardigan even in warm weather, and has trouble even managing the bake sale table at our fundraisers.

Sylvia Parrett's severe style of dress mirrors her approach to life. She and Scoobie butt heads less than they did in the past, but she appreciates his breezy approach to life as much as he appreciates her rigidity. I reminded myself Sylvia *is* dedicated to Harvest for All.

Aretha came to us after Father Jamison found her hanging food pantry signs in laundromats, places she believed would have a lot of people who would use our services. Our other African-American member is the town librarian, Daphne, who went to school with Scoobie and me. Scoobie used to bug the daylights out of her with his obsessive reading of some of the same books. It was a challenge to let others check them out. Scoobie has broadened many aspects of his life since then.

After everyone inquired about our future son or daughter, we settled around the small conference table. Our first orders of business were the ordinary ones – scheduling volunteers for the three half-days we're open each week, making sure the food bank in Lakewood sends us much of what we need, and finding ways to scour grocery stores and volunteer groups for local supplies of food or money to buy it.

Aretha changed topics. "We haven't had a big fundraiser in almost a year. Just the raffle and a couple bake sales."

"And standing in the grocery stores to collect donations," Sylvia said. "Thank goodness for Mr. Markle and the In-Town Grocery Store."

Scoobie grinned. "We haven't had a 'Talk Like a Pirate Day' event in a few years."

"We haven't had any bodies turn up at a fundraiser since then," Sylvia said.

Megan smiled. "Technically it was the night after." Then she dropped the smile, perhaps acknowledging murder is never funny.

"That's true. But before we discuss another fundraiser, I'd like us to talk about someone taking over as chair, at least temporarily."

Silence.

Dr. Welby cleared his throat. "I can help a new person come up to speed, but Myra and I are going to be traveling a lot the next few months."

"I'm sure you'd give a good overview," I said. "Megan, any chance…"

She shook her head. "It's about all I can do to keep track of our volunteers. With Java Jolt and all."

My eyes went to Daphne. "I can do a lot more for a fundraiser, but I'm up for senior librarian."

We all commented that she'd be perfect for the job.

Aretha opened her mouth, but Sylvia sat up straighter and beat her to a comment. "I've been considering whether I could. Now, I can't do it forever, but I think I could provide the continuity we need."

I never really understood the expression 'my heart sank.' "That's really generous of you. You, uh, have the time?"

"At seventy-eight, I don't have a lot on my calendar."

"Good you can still keep track of it," Scoobie said.

Sylvia began to bristle, but she saw his eyebrows go up and down in a Groucho Marx motion. "You behave yourself, Scoobie."

"Yes, ma'am." He carefully avoided looking at me. He knew I had hoped someone else would step forward. I don't see Sylvia as inspiring other volunteers.

"That's settled then," Dr. Welby said. "Sylvia, you can get copies of the files and such from Jolie."

Sylvia nodded. "But I can't devote the time to working in the pantry that Jolie does. I can't stand that long, and I get too impatient sometimes."

Wow. I didn't know she knew herself that well.

Aretha said, "I could do a couple hours one morning a week, but that's all my work schedule would allow."

Megan spoke up. "I've been thinking a lot about that. Maybe we can pay someone for a few hours a week. Since I can't fill in as much as I used to, either."

Scoobie nodded. "I guess we can talk to Harry about whether we have the money for that."

"I bet some of the local churches would do a special collection," Sylvia said, "when we tell them we need extra help for a few months."

There goes my idea of someone taking over permanently.

The meeting broke up after we decided to ask Reverend Jamison to approach Father Teehan about teaming up to talk to the other churches. They seem to work as a sort of tag team, and they goad each other about who can get their congregation to raise more money.

Though I wished someone else had stepped forward, I was grateful to Sylvia. I fell into bed at nine-thirty, but woke from a restless dream before midnight. In my dream, Sylvia wore a pirate hat and brandished a cardboard sword. She ordered a group of frightened bake sale volunteers to sell more brownies or she'd be off with their heads.

CHAPTER TWO

I WOKE UP AT FIVE the next morning because the baby gave a couple of extra-hard kicks. After staring at the ceiling for ten minutes, I crept out of bed. Scoobie didn't have to get up until five-forty-five, and I didn't want to wake him.

I made a cup of caffeine-free coffee and sat in the kitchen to make a list.

- Java Jolt to see what Megan thought of the meeting
- Doctor visit
- Go see cape cod house again with Lester
- Nap
- Get up before Terry gets home from school

I liked our bungalow. I bought it before we married, and it's not far from the center of town, five blocks from the ocean. I got it after Hurricane Sandy. It hadn't sustained too much damage, though it had been somewhat neglected as its prior, elderly owner aged. After a lot of steady maintenance, it's cozy. At this point, I would love a house with two bathrooms and a kitchen that lets me turn around without running into another human or stepping on a cat or skunk.

By the time Scoobie left for the hospital and Terry trudged off to school, I really wanted a nap. I told myself if I felt that way when I got out of the shower I'd hop back into bed. I didn't.

EIGHT-FORTY-FIVE AM WAS too early to go to the obstetrician appointment, so I headed for Java Jolt. I know caffeine is not good for a baby in utero, so I have made a deal with God. Megan is in on it, but Scoobie is not on the need-to-know list.

I order a decaf, and seven-eighths of the cup is just that. Megan puts in a couple of tablespoons of 'real' coffee, and I feel as if I've had something to pep me up. A piece of chocolate candy would have more caffeine.

I felt very out of sorts, and it wasn't all hormones. What if Scoobie lost his job? He'd feel awful, and I wasn't sure I'd know how to make him feel better. We could manage without his income for a while, but we probably wouldn't be able to buy a bigger house.

Maybe we could enclose the back porch. We'd have to even the flooring first, or I'd be sliding from the crib to a rocking chair. I pushed the thought aside. *Think positive. Scoobie won't lose his job.*

I'd been able to park less than a block from the steps that led up to the boardwalk, so I wasn't winded as I passed the colorful, mostly shuttered stores. The uncrowded boardwalk offered sunshine and fifty-five degree April weather, and lifted my spirits. The sound of waves lapping the sand helped, too. In another two weeks, lots of stores would open, at least on the weekends. I suddenly craved cotton candy.

I entered Java Jolt and called to Megan, whose back was to me as she refilled the largest thermos of coffee. "What pastry do you have with no calories?"

She turned her head and smiled. "If I had any of that I'd be rich."

When Megan took over Java Jolt, she didn't have money for major remodeling, but she brightened up the place. She painted the walls a lighter color and also replaced some of the dark-colored tables with a mix of round tables in an oak veneer. Even her light yellow, canvas-type apron sported a beach scene, complete with shells.

Lester Argrow's strong Jersey accent came from the far side of the coffee shop. "Jolie! You wanna get started early?"

Megan grinned and gave me a thumbs up. She hadn't needed to ask what I wanted.

I had been looking forward to a quiet chat with the wise Megan, but it would be rude not to sit with Lester, Ocean Alley's most ornery real estate agent and my friend Ramona's uncle. I patted my tummy and headed toward him. "The baby and I have an ultrasound appointment."

I had begun to understand the cliché about a house bursting at the seams, and we hadn't even put together any of the baby furniture. As annoying as he could be, I had to admit Lester had worked hard to find us not just a bigger place, but one that fit our budget.

The four-bedroom cape cod had large rooms, a huge kitchen, and lots of light. The best part was its location – three blocks from the ocean, next to Aunt Madge's Cozy Corner B&B. She and Harry will be our baby's surrogate grandparents. Plus, I've loved Aunt Madge with all my heart for all my life.

Lester, always uncomfortable talking about my pregnancy, set down his mug, slopping some onto the table. He grabbed a balled-up napkin and dabbed at it. "Uh, that's good. Scoobie going with you?"

"He was supposed to meet me there for the last part, to talk to the doctor, but his boss says the hospital is looking to cut a position from Radiology. We decided he shouldn't leave."

Lester seems to think a loud voice makes up for his short stature. "What, the bozos won't give him a half-hour off?"

Megan approached with my coffee. "You know, Lester, if you call doctors bozos and they have to operate on you…"

Lester waved a hand, and Megan handed him a couple of napkins. "I meant the lughead Scoobie works for, not the docs."

Megan winked at me and walked away.

"His boss said he could go, but we decided that the day after Sam said the hospital was considering getting rid of a position wasn't the day to be gone. I have several more appointments after this."

"Huh." Lester switched tacks faster than a sailboat in thirty-knot winds. "So, you ready to make a final decision when we get together at one?"

"I'll need to talk to Scoob…"

"Scoobie said it's up to you."

I frowned. "When did he tell you that?" Scoobie had told me the same thing, but I figured he was trying to keep Lester from bugging him.

"I called him at the hospital yesterday."

Okay, he needed Lester off the phone. Nice of him to remember to tell me.

"He wants me to be sure I'm okay with having two of the bedrooms upstairs."

"Didn't you say the baby'd be on the same floor as youse?"

I nodded. "Yes, and Terry says he's okay being upstairs, but we'd have to carry towels and clothes down to the laundry, and…"

He waved a hand again. "That's what the guys are for. Plus, you could put in a laundry chute, maybe going down along the heating ducts."

There was no talking to Lester when he was in full sales mode. He'd try to get a clam to upgrade to a bigger shell. "I like it. But you can't follow me from room to room jabbering when we look at it this afternoon."

"So, if you do the appraisal you can maybe get a better price."

Megan giggled from behind the counter, but Lester didn't notice.

"Lester! Do you know how unethical that would be?"

"Oh, well, maybe. So, Harry gonna do it?"

I shook my head. "He said if a bank asked us to do the appraisal, he'd tell them to go to Stenner's." Jennifer Stenner inherited the town's much larger real estate appraisal firm her grandfather founded.

Lester fumed, "That dame charges more."

"I know she's told you not to call her a dame." I looked at my watch. "Oops. I don't want to be late for the photography session."

"What about…?" he began.

I stood. "You want me to bring a copy of the sonogram image to show you at one?"

Lester reddened. "No, no. I can wait for the Polaroids."

I left Lester to his coffee and headed out the door, almost running headlong into a short man who walked with his head down. "Good morning, Max. Are you here to help Megan or look for broken muffin pieces?"

Max touched his stomach, which was perhaps an inch or two rounder than a year ago. Not that much.

"Here to be careful, be careful."

I am not bothered by Max's speech patterns, which are the result of a severe traumatic brain injury sustained during a U.S. war with Iraq. He's able to live independently because people like Scoobie and I help him manage the aspects of his life that overwhelm him.

"You look good, Max."

"Okay, just okay. I can't put on any more pounds. More pounds."

Max reached for the Java Jolt door handle. "I refill the napkin holders and sweep the floor. The floor."

Before I could say goodbye, he had entered the store and called out to Megan. Max is considerate, but he'll never get an A for social graces.

DOCTOR MADISON WAS RUNNING behind, so I read a full issue of *Parenting Today* in her waiting room. I worried constantly that we would flub up. Or I would. My parents loved my sister Renée and me, but Mom would be called overbearing by anyone's definition. And kind of self-centered. Would I be like that?

Scoobie wished he'd grown up differently. His awful mother never knew where he was, or cared. He spent occasional time with Aunt Madge even before he met me. She never had kids, but even a little time with her helped him become who he is.

Would I always be a generous enough soul to put the baby first? I knew Scoobie would. And he always said how grateful he was that I'd immediately warmed to Terry and tried to make him the center of our little universe these last few months. I tell Scoobie not to thank me. Some days are unpredictable, but mostly it's a joy to have Terry with us.

The door to the exam rooms opened and Gina grinned. "Come on back, Jolie."

She worked at Silver Times Senior Living when Aunt Madge briefly stayed there. She likes the hours better in the doctor's office.

I followed her into an exam room, and she pointed to a chair. Gina isn't a nurse. She takes blood pressure and such before the nurse comes in. Then the doctor. Kind of a medical parade. Plus, today I would have an ultrasound. I'd had one at what we thought was nineteen weeks. Today should be week thirty-two. Or maybe thirty-three. Scoobie and I had not been very precise.

My sister kept wanting me to have another one before this, but I asked the doctor if it was safe to wait. A friend in Lakewood had several, and she'd pull out the images and wave them in front of my face. I always wanted to say I'd wait for the bassinet version.

A few strands of Gina's thick, black hair had trouble staying in her bun as she tightened the blood pressure cuff. She frowned and I saw my numbers were higher than usual.

"I have to deal with Lester after this. I must have been thinking about that."

Gina laughed. "Breath quietly for ten seconds."

I did and she checked it again. Lower.

By the time the ultrasound technician, Sarah, came in wheeling her equipment, I'd answered two sets of questions. She made round three, though she was mostly being conversational as she got her equipment set up.

She'd barely started moving the three-inch device over the cold jelly on my stomach when she kind of jerked to a stop and started up again.

"You okay?" I asked.

She kept her eyes on the screen. "Thought I was going to sneeze. Made the transducer jump a little." She smiled, still focused on the screen. "The cold device on your tummy."

In an almost absent-minded tone, she asked what was new in our world. I told her that we were about to buy a cape cod house, and how great it was that we'd be next door to Aunt Madge and Harry.

"How many bedrooms?"

"Four. We could do with three, but it has two upstairs, plus another bathroom. We'll be set for life."

"Always good to have room to grow." Sarah stowed the transducer. "Let me get you wiped off here. Doctor'll be in right away."

I started to sit up. "Can I see?"

She put a hand on my shoulder. "You know how Dr. Madison likes to give all the news. She'll be right in."

She made a cursory pass at the jelly on the belly, as Scoobie calls it, and I watched Sarah's back as she shut the door. *Should I be worried? Did she see something bad?* I pushed the thought aside. I felt good. The result of the ultrasound, the sonogram, would show the baby was fine.

The door opened and Dr. Madison came in. "Hello Jolie. Looking good." She made for the machine.

"That's great. When Sarah left so quickly I thought something was wrong."

"Oh, no…Scoobie coming?"

I sat up fast. "What? What is it?"

She smiled and spoke gently. "Nothing bad. When we first met, you and Scoobie talked about maybe having two children. How would you like to do that in one fell swoop?"

For several seconds, Dr. Madison continued to talk, but I didn't hear what she said. My brain had a sort of white sound noise. "Wait, what? How do you know there're two babies?"

I shivered through the conversation with Dr. Madison. Apparently it's rare, but even at nineteen weeks a smaller twin can "play con artist" and hide behind the larger one. She had not heard two heartbeats.

Dr. Madison stopped talking and regarded me. "Really, I think I should call Scoobie."

I shook my head again. "It's not that I'm unhappy about it. It's just, just that I need a few minutes." I tried not to cry. Tears of joy, of course.

"It's natural to be overwhelmed. You've had a lot of changes the last few months. It will all work out." Dr. Madison smiled.

You can come over and change two sets of diapers at two AM. "I know, and Scoobie will be thrilled." Terry's face came to mind. "And so will his brother Terry."

"I'm sure Terry will be a big help," she said, gently. "For him, it'll be like having a brother and sister."

"You're sure one is a boy?"

"Anatomy never lies. At least not in that direction." She peered at the screen. "You guys weren't sure of the exact date of conception. I think you might be ahead of what we thought. I'd say...thirty three, maybe thirty-four weeks."

"That's good, right? We aim for thirty-seven?"

"Yes. Twins can be early, but these two don't show signs of making an immediate appearance."

They better not show up early. "Plenty of time to buy two of everything." I tried to sound confident.

Dr. Madison patted my hand. "You'll do great."

"I'll tell Scoobie and Terry when they get home, about three-thirty. Maybe Scoobie and I can come by or call you later, to talk to you together?"

"Perfect. I don't expect any deliveries this afternoon. Call any time before six, or tomorrow afternoon."

I tried to sound enthusiastic. "Sounds good."

Dr. Madison left the room and I dressed while I waited for Sarah to make copies of the image of our two babies. *Two babies!!!!*

I chided myself. I was simply scared. I would love these babies. Two healthy babies at age thirty-two!

We weren't rich, but we would be okay. Scoobie's father had divided his veteran's life insurance between Terry and Scoobie. We called our portion "the baby's college fund." Now it would be for two. *Oh my God. College!*

The door opened and Gina entered, smiling broadly. She shut the door, walked the few paces, and grabbed me in a hug. "I'm so happy for you. And Aunt Madge will just burst with joy."

Aunt Madge's image came to me. Octogenarian that she is, she lay on the floor with both of her retrievers trying to lick her face as she laughed and tried to avoid their tongues.

I felt my heart slow and smiled to myself. Aunt Madge has soft white hair, which she regularly dyes with temporary colors. In my mind, she had what my father one time called her skunk hair – black with a white streak. She never used the combination again.

I pulled back from the hug and smiled. "It's a lot to absorb, but it will all be fine."

"I saw Lester at the grocery store. He said he's selling you a good house."

Good heavens, Lester. I nodded slowly. "If he finds out he'll push for a bigger one."

Gina's eyes widened. "I would never tell anyone."

"Silly. I know that." I picked up my purse. "I think we have a lot to do."

I WAS NOT IN THE mood to look at the house again, but if I canceled Lester would call Scoobie and Scoobie would think something was wrong. I didn't want to go to Java Jolt. Megan would be able to tell I was going bonkers. She and Scoobie both tell me not to play poker.

I wasn't ready to talk to anyone besides family just yet. Mostly I was afraid I'd cry. I knew I was happy. I knew it. But I still felt as if my composure might crack mid-sentence. *Get a grip. There's nothing to be afraid of.*

I opted for Arnie's Diner, which has a kind of pictorial history of Ocean Alley on its walls. One even has Uncle Gordon, Aunt Madge's late husband, and his wooden flat-bottom boat. Aunt Madge still has the boat in the back of her garage.

I ordered scrambled eggs and toast.

Arnie eyed me after he wrote down my order. "You feeling okay?"

"Just tired. So much to do."

He reached down to pat my hand. "You and Scoobie, you'll be great parents."

If only I could believe that.

AUNT MADGE'S NEIGHBORS WERE not home when Lester and I went through the house again. Which was good, because Lester kept pointing out things he thought needed to be repaired or replaced.

Finally, I stopped and turned to face him. "Lester, you usually want people to offer high for a house. It's like you're giving us reasons to low-ball the offer."

"Yeah." Since we weren't in a restaurant, he chomped on the unlit cigar he often has at the corner of his mouth. "You want the house, so I want youse guys to be able to buy it. The asking price is maybe high."

"You know their decision to accept will be based on what they want, not what we have. Besides," I rubbed the top of my baby bump, "you already told us what we should be able to get for our place. We'll be okay."

"I can bring a contract over tonight and you and Scoobie…"

"Not tonight." Realizing how abrupt I sounded, I added, "We want to make Terry part of the decision. Tomorrow would be better, and we'll have time to discuss it." While this was true, Terry had already pronounced the house "close enough to Aunt Madge to be good."

CHAPTER THREE

I HAD NEVER FELT SUCH a mix of happy and scared. Especially after looking at the house, I really wanted to go to the hospital to tell Scoobie. But I didn't think my stomach would take the odor mix of alcohol and Lysol that permeates the place. Plus, we sure wouldn't have any privacy.

I intended to go straight home after I left Lester, but decided to stop by Mr. Markle's In-Town Grocery, near the courthouse. I would buy a pre-made cake as well as some pink and blue icing to write something —what?— on the cake. Perhaps "you better sit down" in alternating colors.

At two-fifteen I pulled into our small driveway and hauled my tired self up the short flight of steps. I put the pound cake and packages of pink and blue decorating icing on the coffee table, with a couple of pieces of mail covering them. I didn't make it to the bedroom before I fell asleep.

At three-fifteen Terry ran up the porch steps and almost banged the front door open. He caught it before it hit the wall. Pebbles had been about to walk toward the door to greet him, but quickly waddled back to her spot under his bed.

I sat up fast and stared as he dug a piece of paper from the pocket of his jeans. For a couple of seconds I felt dizzy, but it passed.

"I have a stupid note for you."

I kept my tone light and held out my hand. "I'd been hoping for a smart one."

"You won't get it from Assistant Principal Rosen." Terry sat at the other end of the couch, and reached down to pet Jazz.

I gulped internally and a baby kicked hard. Rosen had held that job at the high school when I lived with Aunt Madge at her B&B during my junior year. I wouldn't call him narrow-minded, but he thought rules were paramount. He and Scoobie had rarely seen eye-to-eye when Scoobie was in high school.

The sealed envelope was addressed to Scoobie O'Brien and Jolie Gentil. I met Terry's gaze. "Do you know what it says?"

"I know the subject matter."

I patted the cushion next to mine. "Let's read it together."

"Sure." He slid down next to me. Jazz hopped on his lap mid slide, planting herself firmly in place. Terry gently loosened her claws from his jeans.

I slit the envelope with my thumb, unfolded the letter, and held it so we could both see.

April 28

Dear Scoobie and Jolie,

I wanted to make you aware of a situation that developed late today. As you know, Terry shares a locker at Ocean Alley Middle School with Eddie Matlock. At the end of the day, Eddie reported that a sum of cash had "vanished" (his word) from the shared locker.

I thought I knew where the letter was going, and glanced at Terry. "Was it a lot?"

"Eddie says so. I never saw it."

I went back to the letter.

We can make no judgment at this time about the circumstances or the amount of cash that may have been removed. Eddie reports that he is missing $82. As you know, this is more than students are supposed to have with them in the building.

My heart lightened somewhat. Mr. Rosen said he could make no judgment.

However, Eddie has alleged that he and Terry had been arguing recently, and he asked that I examine the locker and Terry's person.

My stomach clenched. "Did you give him permission to search your locker and pockets?"

Terry scowled. "They can search our lockers anytime. It's school property. I pulled out my pockets, which had no cash, and I told him if he wanted a cavity search we were done talking."

If Scoobie had been here, the brothers would have high-fived. On a TV sit-com that would be a good line. When talking to the middle school assistant principal for discipline, it probably hadn't gone over well.

I went back to the letter.

I would appreciate it if one or both of you would accompany Terry to school tomorrow. Over Eddie's objections, I have asked his parents to do the same. We will meet separately. I suggest eight-fifteen, which is just after the start of first period.

Rosen phrased his order as a request, but we would certainly be there. Scoobie would not be happy. His day at the Ocean Alley Hospital Radiology Department started at seven AM. He wouldn't be mad at Terry, but he would be angry that the hospital would have to get someone to cover his shift on short notice.

I refolded the letter and laid it next to me on the sofa. "Of course you didn't take any money."

Terry's shoulders relaxed. "If he even had any. Eddie never has cash."

"I don't know Eddie well. Can you think of why he would make such an outrageous accusation?"

Terry stood, holding Jazz. "I'm going to grab an apple and some chips while we talk."

I made to get up and he laughed. "Stay there. You want anything?"

"Maybe an apple." As he walked across the living room to our narrow kitchen, I thought he had grown a lot more relaxed than he was ten minutes ago. Had he been worried we wouldn't believe him?

More steps on the porch announced Scoobie. His somber expression told me he'd heard more information, or at least rumors, about layoffs at the hospital. He raised his eyebrows briefly and tilted his head toward the kitchen. I nodded.

"Hey you two," he called. "Pebbles' favorite person is home."

Terry called from the kitchen. "Wrong."

Scoobie came over to me and rumpled my hair as he sat next to me. "Good day?"

I kept my tone light. "The usual rumpus." I lowered my voice. "Terry's had some stuff at school."

Terry came back in from the kitchen, apple in hand. "My day stunk."

I picked the letter off of the couch, where I had placed it face-down. "Assistant Principal Rosen sent a letter, but the tone tells me he doubts all the circumstances described."

Scoobie took the letter, read for fifteen seconds, and tossed it on the table. "Yeah, for Rosen it's a good tone." He pointed at Terry. "And of course it's a crock."

Terry sat on the rocker and sighed. "But everybody'll hear about it."

That's why he's seemed so worried. "It won't be fun, but it'll get resolved quickly."

Terry jerked his thumb behind him, in the direction of the front door. "Wanna go for a walk?"

Would I never get a chance to tell Scoobie? I tried to look serious. "Gee, I'm tuckered."

Scoobie laughed and Terry looked stricken.

"Just kidding. I know you meant a guys' walk. Jazz and I prefer some quiet time."

Jazz followed the brothers out the door.

CHAPTER FOUR

I MUST HAVE FALLEN asleep as soon as they left.

Terry's voice woke me. "You are alive, aren't you?"

I had ended up on my side, on the couch. I opened my eyes slightly. "I need three more hours of sleep."

Terry laughed. "If there were two of you you'd have time."

My eyes flew open, sort of double wide. *Two of me! I'm going to have twins.*

Terry stood above me. "So, you look alive now, but kind of demented."

I was afraid he'd read my mind, fragmented though it was. I needed to gather my thoughts. "Will you bring me some iced tea?"

"Sure." He turned toward the kitchen and opened the fridge.

Scoobie sat next to me and spoke softly. "You look kind of frazzled. I think the thing with Terry will work out."

"I know. I wanted to tell you as soon as you got home, but I wanted to let Terry talk to you." I looked at the coffee table and removed the mail I'd placed on top of the cake.

Scoobie frowned, clearly perplexed. Then his gaze followed mine to the table. He took in the cake and the pink and blue frostings.

I turned to meet his eyes. "We have some big news." I had been determined to be unendingly cheerful, but my voice shook. "Would you like to see an image of both of your children?"

Scoobie sat completely still, his eyes locked with mine.

Terry ran in from the kitchen, jumped up, whooped, and started a jerky sort of dance around the living room.

I whispered to Scoobie. "You think it's too much?"

He pulled me to him, my head on his shoulder, his chin on my head. "I can't believe we got this lucky." He pushed me back. "They're both okay? Wait, are you okay?"

"Besides being totally panic-stricken, I'm fine."

He finally grinned. "Two for the price of one. Where's the sonogram image?"

I smiled. "I'm sure we'll get a bill for both." I reached for the small brown envelope, which was in my purse on the coffee table, and pulled it out.

Scoobie grabbed it, took out the four-by-six image, and held it up to the light streaming through the window. Terry crowded behind him. I stayed seated.

"Man, there really are two," Terry said.

Scoobie turned to me. "Does it matter that one is smaller?"

I shook my head. "Dr. Madison said it's not uncommon, and they'll be a lot closer to the same size when they're born, probably."

"The last time you only saw the bigger one?" Terry asked.

"Yes. Dr. Madison says the larger one is likely a girl."

"Yeah," Terry said. "I remember they said they couldn't be one-hundred percent sure last time."

Scoobie pointed to a spot on the image. "And this is clearly a boy. Remember what I told you, Terry?"

Terry looked over his shoulder and grinned at me. "He said any boy of his would be really obvious in the picture."

Scoobie spread his thumb and index finger apart. "I mean, readily apparent." He grinned at me.

I laughed at how alike they were. "You guys are too much."

Then I thought of a question I'd meant to ask Terry several times. We had almost no photos of Scoobie as a child. Aunt Madge had found a couple pictures at his elementary school, but nothing when he was a toddler or younger. "Terry, where are your baby pictures?"

He frowned. "I'm pretty sure Dad put them in one of the boxes he packed." He gave Scoobie a questioning look, and I did the same.

He shrugged. "I went through all of it. Maybe I missed something. I'll check. Are they in an album?"

"Yep. You'll find them." Terry stared again at the sonogram images.

A thought formed. Family friends had hoped to adopt Terry, and were disappointed that Terence brought him to us. Could they have the photos?

Scoobie sent Terry into the kitchen to take some frozen lasagna from the freezer and turn on the oven. Smart young man that Terry is, he stayed out there.

I reached for Scoobie's hand, and we settled into the couch, both of us with feet on the coffee table. "Can you believe this?"

Scoobie's expression darkened. "I just thought...is this safe for you? Will they do a caesarian? You didn't want one."

"Oh, I forgot. Dr. Madison said we could call any time before six, or tomorrow. So we can talk to her together."

His brow unfurrowed. "Guess we need to think of questions." He raised an eyebrow. "Did you tell Aunt Madge?"

"No! I didn't even go to Java Jolt after the doctor because I was afraid that Megan would be able to tell something was different."

"You want to invite Madge and Harry over here?"

I shook my head slowly. "She has to give bread and tea to her B&B guests in a few minutes. And I think I'd like us to go to the Cozy Corner. That way I won't feel like we have to entertain. I'm so tired."

Terry's head stuck around the kitchen doorjamb. "Can I come?"

I pointed a finger at him.

"I promise I wasn't listening. But you said Aunt Madge…"

Scoobie kissed my cheek. "In this house, secrets are hard. I forgot to ask if you made a decision about the house."

Terry came into the living room. All that mattered to him was that it was next to the B&B. "I liked it."

I nodded. "I did, too. I told Lester we'd call him tomorrow. He said the owners are ready to start packing as soon as we sign the contract."

Terry took his place in the rocker again. "Can you call him tonight?"

Scoobie raised an eyebrow at me.

"I'm really tired, and I think we need to tell a few people this evening. Aunt Madge won't blab, but once you tell one person…"

"Yeah," Scoobie said. "We don't want George or Megan to hear from someone else."

I thought of our high school artist friend. "Or Ramona. We need to tell her at the same time as George, or before."

Scoobie seemed amused. "Why is that?"

"Sometimes she reminds me we knew her first." George was a year ahead of us in high school, and I had only vague memories of him as a kind of bossy photographer for the school paper.

Ramona and I had geometry together. I sometimes tripped over her art portfolio. Her image came to mind. Dressed in her sort of modern hippie garb, she fulfills a lot of artist stereotypes. Perhaps more pragmatic than some.

"Can I tell people at school?" Terry asked.

"Could you wait one day?" Scoobie asked. "Except maybe your buddy Kevin, if you make him swear not to talk about it."

I SAT AT THE KITCHEN table, slicing and buttering a loaf of Italian bread that we would have with the lasagna. Scoobie's and my conversation with Dr. Madison had been brief. She was confident that the babies were a good weight, and she reassured Scoobie, twice, that delivering two babies wouldn't be hard for a woman as fit as I am.

Now we had to come up with two names. Before we talked about names a few weeks ago, I sensed Terry had an unspoken question. Finally, he casually asked what the child's (now children's'!) last name would be. Scoobie and I had discussed it. Terry's name was O'Brien, the same as Scoobie's. The baby would be more like his sibling. The names had to be O'Brien.

Truth be told, one reason I kept my maiden name was because my dad had girls, and the name would vanish if I changed it. Of course, it would anyway because our kids would be O'Briens. But, my choice made my dad happy.

I became aware of Scoobie and Terry, who were talking animatedly in the living room. Terry's voice grew more exuberant. He had already planned to use one of the two upstairs bedrooms, but knowing we were about to sign the contract on the house made it more real. He thought he and Scoobie should buy two cribs so they could start putting them together before we moved.

Before I could jump in, Scoobie said it would be easier to wait, so we didn't have to move them.

I smiled to myself. We had all been happy about the baby, but now that everything seemed to be coming together at once, concentration had begun to focus on getting ready for the babies. Just now, my big focus was on staying awake long enough to talk to Aunt Madge and Harry.

I could tell that Aunt Madge knew something was up as soon as I called to ask if we could come over after supper. Aunt Madge would know how I felt. Happy, scared, overwhelmed. I wanted to practice my cheerful expression, the one that said I'm so thrilled I can't stand it.

The timer dinged. Before I could stand up, Scoobie called from the living room. "I'll get that pan out of the oven. It's too heavy for you."

I called to him, "Yesterday you would have let me pick it up."

He came into the kitchen. "Yesterday we had only one baby."

Terry laughed. "They were both there, you just didn't know it."

I didn't eat much, probably because of all the excitement.

We made a cursory pass at tidying the kitchen, and Terry said he wanted to call Aunt Madge before we walked over. I didn't need to ask him what he talked to her about. Once Scoobie had said, during dinner, that it would be tough for him to call off for the morning, Terry wanted reinforcements.

In his quest to know more about his new family, Terry searched the newspaper archives this winter. There've been a couple of awkward photos of me in the *Ocean Alley Press*, courtesy of former reporter George Winters.

I'm pretty sure the one that bothers Terry the most is from the 10th high school reunion, when I stuck out my tongue. Or the one that showed me loading excess food into plastic bags. Bottom line, Terry seemed concerned that Rosen wouldn't take me seriously.

From what I gathered after the call, Aunt Madge was perfect. She didn't let herself be drawn into something she knew I could handle, with or without Scoobie, and she apparently reassured Terry. I doubted she would even discuss it with him when we got to the B&B.

When Terry finished talking to Aunt Madge, we grabbed jackets and headed out. Terry walked ahead, occasionally turning back and gesturing that we should hurry up.

"You go ahead," Scoobie called. "Aunt Madge probably has a brownie waiting for you."

The Cozy Corner is on D Street, three blocks from the ocean. In the 1930s it was four blocks, but the great Atlantic Hurricane of 1944 wiped out the boardwalk and A Street. It's why Aunt Madge wouldn't look any closer to the shore when she was shopping for a B&B after Uncle Gordon died when I was five.

We reached D Street, and Terry ran across the small parking lot beside the B&B, and jogged up the steps. A yawn escaped me. "I wish I had his energy."

Scoobie put his arm around my shoulders and I rested my head on his shoulder for a moment. "Sometimes I forget that he's only eleven. He acts so mature."

Scoobie nodded. "Listen, because I know you'll probably go to sleep as soon as we get back home, is there anything else I should know about Terry and this Eddie kid?"

"I will of course be on Terry's side 100 percent tomorrow. But I have a nagging feeling that Eddie has some problems at home. I mean, why even have money in a locker beyond what he needs for school? Is he hiding it from his family?"

"We can wonder, but I don't think we can ask him." Scoobie gave me a sideways glance. "You agree?"

"If we weren't about to have twins, I'd want to pay more attention. But I'm pretty preoccupied."

Scoobie laughed and touched the back my head. "That's an understatement."

As we walked up the side porch steps toward the open door, we could hear Terry's animated conversation with Aunt Madge, though we couldn't hear the exact words. In part this was because they were almost drowned out by the welcome from

Aunt Madge's exuberant retrievers, Mr. Rogers and Miss Piggy.

Scoobie turned his head toward me. "He's so excited. You think he'll tell Madge and Harry before we do?"

"Not directly. In fact, she may think he's excited because he's worried about school." I grasped the railing. I was beginning to feel like someone who had run a half marathon carrying a twenty-pound weight. In a way, I had.

Harry greeted us at the door and winked as he opened it. "I didn't follow the entire narration, but I gather he's concerned about tomorrow."

I shrugged out of my jacket and hung it on one of the pegs Harry had recently installed by the door. "We hope it goes well."

Scoobie clapped Harry on the shoulder. Then he crossed the breakfast room toward the swinging door that led to their great room, with its kitchen at one end and the sliding door to the back yard at the other. Over his shoulder, Scoobie asked, "Did he tell you we have more news?" He kept moving.

Harry pecked my cheek. "Not that I heard." His eyes held a question.

I smiled. "If I tell you first it'll hurt her fee…"

Terry's voice carried from the kitchen. "Scoobie. Can we tell it's twins now?"

Scoobie laughed. "I guess we have."

Harry grabbed me in a hug and Aunt Madge shot out of the kitchen with her arms outstretched. "Oh, my word. Is it true?"

I leaned into her embrace, and finally had my cry.

After Scoobie replaced Aunt Madge in the hug and comfort role, we trooped back to the great room.

I insisted my tears were those of joy. "Really, it's all good."

Eyes wide, Terry moved pillows on the love seat so I could sit. "I'm sorry, Jolie, it just came out."

I blew him a kiss. "I hadn't figured out exactly what to say, so you did me, us, a favor."

Miss Piggy sat on my foot and Mister Rogers tried to head butt her so she would move. He finally gave up and settled next to her.

Scoobie squeezed my shoulder as he sat next to me. "We're really happy. It's just a lot to plan for."

Aunt Madge sat a plate of brownies on the coffee table in front of us. "And in a relatively short time. How did they miss a baby?"

I let Scoobie recount how the small twin – whom he assured Madge and Harry would 'catch up' – had been hidden by his larger sister in a prior ultrasound.

Terry had continued to sit very still, frowning and red-faced. I pointed at the brownies. "I'm not mad. You can eat one for me."

He brightened, "Thanks," and dove into rapid chatter about how he and Scoobie would put together two cribs and that it would be okay to store diapers in his room if there were too many for the babies' room.

Harry placed an ice bucket with a corked bottle next to the brownies. "We had this apple cider champagne planned for delivery day, but this is too good an opportunity to pass up." He grinned at me. "I take it I'll be doing solo real estate appraisals a little longer than we thought."

I leaned back into the loveseat. "You never know. I might need breaks early. Scoobie can be in charge."

Aunt Madge gave a ladylike snort. "Anytime they're sleeping you'll want to nap." She met my gaze. "Of course, I probably know a couple of people who will volunteer to watch them."

"Ramona will," Terry said.

Scoobie grinned. "And George."

I sat up straighter. "Over my dead body."

He held his hands up in mock surrender. "Just kidding." More seriously, he added, "He can help me."

"Make sure you let him diaper the little boy," Aunt Madge said.

I hid a smile behind the drink of sparkling cider Harry had just given me. "It's a deal."

"Why the boy?" Terry asked.

Harry, a grandfather several times over, said, dryly, "I'll tell you later. So," he took in first Scoobie and then me. "Do you have names?"

We each shook our heads. "Renée said they had ideas for their girls, but they didn't pick names until they saw each one."

I suddenly felt more relaxed. My sister would be a huge help.

CHAPTER FIVE

TERRY AND I LEFT THE house at seven forty-five the next morning. There aren't too many visitor parking spaces at the middle school, and I didn't want to lumber too far to get to Rosen's office. I also wanted a quick exit.

I glanced at Terry, next to me on the front seat. From his stoic expression, I knew he wished Aunt Madge had joined us. "Is there anything in particular you want me to say or not say?"

He turned his head toward me and I sensed the beginning of a smile. "You mean that's all it would take to control what you say?"

"I'm trying not to embarrass you. If you prefer…"

"No, that's good," he said, quickly. Then he thought for a moment. "I guess I know you'll let Rosen know you believe me."

"Of course."

"I don't like calling Eddie a liar, but I've never seen him with that kind of money. And I don't get why he would blame me for anything. We usually get along."

"But you don't hang out beyond school, right?"

Terry shook his head. "He's not a friend like Kevin, but we get along okay."

I thought Kevin initially spent time with Terry because his uncle, Sergeant Morehouse of the Ocean Alley Police, asked him to. The boys bonded over soccer.

I turned on the Toyota's blinker, made a left into the middle school parking lot, and snagged the last visitor spot. I turned off the ignition and twisted toward Terry. "Do you have your game face on?"

He rolled his eyes. "You're trying too hard."

As we walked toward the main entrance, I moved at waddle pace. Even though my five-foot-six frame was the same except for the beach ball in the front, I found it hard to walk quickly. *You're in your early thirties. Pregnancy is not that big a deal for a woman your age.*

Terry opened the heavy exterior door. "Do you have gas or something?"

"Are you saying I stink?"

"No. Your expression looks like you hurt."

"I'm fine." I paused at the security desk to sign the visitor log.

The elderly, African-American guard had known Aunt Madge for decades, and commented on my shape every time I saw him. "You're getting there, Mrs. Scoobie."

"Can't come soon enough, Mr. Evans."

"Heh, heh. My daughter said the exact thing before her last two. You got a name?"

I shook my head. "Not yet." I gave him my four-fingered wave and didn't say the idea of two babies at once was blowing my mind.

School had been in session for twelve minutes, so the locker-strewn halls had grown quiet. The Ocean Alley Middle School office was only about fifty yards from the entrance, and I could tell Terry wanted to walk faster. I wanted a potty break, but decided I could hold it.

A tall counter faced us and a woman at a desk behind it scribbled furiously on a chart of some sort. She looked up, unsmiling. "Hello you two, you're early."

Not a warm welcome. "I never know how long it'll take me to get from point A to point B."

Her frown relaxed, and the woman I knew to be Mrs. Klinger nodded her bobbed head. "Have a seat. Mr. Rosen should be out for you in about ten minutes." She tilted her head toward the six-foot, fabric-covered partition behind her, which separated the short hallway of administrative offices from the open waiting area.

Though 'waiting area' would be too generous a term. Five hard, plastic chairs were grouped in a corner because there would not have been room to move if they had been spread around the narrow space across from the counter.

Terry and I settled in, with me doing my best to appear graceful. "Do you have anything after school?" I asked.

"I'm supposed to do homework at Kevin's house. I'm helping him with his geometry."

"I didn't know you took that."

"I don't. I like it."

"That's just wrong," I said.

Terry's laugh was genuine. "I heard you say you hated it. Scoobie said when I take it next year I can teach you every night."

I started to say he could tell Scoobie he'd have to change a lot more diapers if I had to do math, but the door to what I knew to be Rosen's office opened. His voice carried to us. "I want to thank you for coming in this morning, Mr. and Mrs. Matlock, Eddie."

Terry and I looked at each other. We hadn't said so, but we both seemed to have assumed that since we were scheduled at eight-fifteen we would meet with Rosen first. Terry sat up straighter and I made a failed attempt to better straddle the small chair.

Mrs. Klinger worked hard not to notice that opposing sides were about to see each other. Terry looked away, apparently not wanting to meet Eddie's eyes. He needn't have worried. Eddie studied the floor intently as he walked past us and out the door. I thought his stern-looking father seemed angry and his mother -- a rumpled forty-something with graying black hair -- appeared confused.

A bell tinkled as the glass door swung shut behind them. I hadn't noticed the bell earlier, but Terry hadn't jerked the door open the way Mr. Matlock did. I didn't think the three of them had even noticed us.

After five seconds of silence, Mrs. Klinger walked behind the partition, likely to tell Rosen we had arrived.

I looked at Terry and spoke barely above a whisper. "They don't look happy."

He nodded, but said nothing.

Mrs. Klinger returned. "It'll just be a minute."

I wondered if I had time to use the bathroom, and decided not. I wished I could cross my legs.

Rosen came from behind the partition. He looked from me to Terry and back to me, unsmiling.

I stood. "Short notice for Scoobie to take off work. His hospital shift starts at seven."

Rosen's eyebrows went up. "Of course. I was thinking early would let families come in before work, but I should have remembered he's out at the hospital." He gestured we should follow him. "X-ray, right?"

"Radiology," Terry said, quite firmly.

It came across almost as a rebuke, and I cringed, inwardly. "If necessary, you can call him after about three-thirty."

We had reached his office and he pointed to three reasonably comfortable chairs across from his desk. "Doubt I'll need to, but he can certainly call me."

As we sat, Rosen asked, "When's the big day?" He smiled, rare for him. "Not soon enough for you?"

I thought he was trying to put us at ease, and I smiled back. "I am counting the days."

Rosen faced Terry. "I needed to talk to you and Eddie with your families because Eddie's allegations were pretty serious. You want to tell me anything before I talk more?"

Terry nodded. "Lately, he's been...I guess we've both been kind of...off with each other. He said he thought I put stuff on his shelf. I didn't. But we didn't have it out or anything."

"Did you ever, even earlier in the year, see money in the locker?"

Terry shrugged. "Just a couple of quarters. I've seen him go into the laundromat to grab a soda from the machine. After school."

"You guys walk home together?" Rosen asked.

Terry shook his head. "We leave the building about the same time, but we don't, like, walk together."

"I get that." Rosen sighed. "These he-said-she-said, or I guess he-said-he-said in this case, accusations are tough. Add to that that neither of you have ever been in trouble, and it's a challenge."

"I didn't take any money," Terry said.

Rosen nodded, but his expression did not change.

I shifted in my seat. Rosen glanced at me and almost smiled. I knew he was thinking of times he had called Scoobie to the office, or even suspended him, when Rosen worked at the high school.

He met Terry's eyes. "Your brother and I would occasionally butt heads, but I think he would tell you I try to play fair."

"He did."

Now I know what they talked about on their walk last night.

Rosen picked up a pencil and tapped the eraser end on his blotter. "I'm not giving much away when I tell you Eddie's parents had no idea he kept cash in his locker. Or the amount."

"So, they didn't know how much?" Terry asked.

"That's between Eddie and his parents," Rosen said.

Terry's face reddened. "Did he even tell them how much?"

"Again..." Rosen began and stopped for a moment. "You can probably tell Scoobie and Jolie almost anything, can't you?"

Terry nodded.

My teeth had begun to float and I shifted in my seat.

Rosen eyed me. "Faculty restroom is two doors down."

I can move really fast when I don't want to pee my pants. Fortunately, the door to the single-stall bathroom stood open and I was able to do my business and get back to Rosen's office quickly.

Rosen nodded to me, and I said, "I'm really sorry."

Terry surprised me by grinning broadly. "Next time I'll see if you need to potty before we leave."

Rosen's laugh was explosive, and took me by surprise. And definitely Terry. *Glad I'm always good for a laugh.*

As I settled in my now comfortable seat, he sobered. "Terry and I have been talking. There is no easy resolution here, but my instinct says Terry did not steal any money from Eddie."

I figured he had said this to Terry while I was gone, because Terry did not appear surprised.

Rosen pointed to each of us. "This is not for anyone's ears except you two and Scoobie, understood?"

Terry and I nodded and he said, "Yes, sir."

"I told Eddie that where he got any money was none of my business, but it would help if he could elaborate some on that. Because I need some indication there was money in the locker."

Without thinking, I asked, "Could he?"

Rosen shrugged. "He wasn't willing to in front of his parents."

As angry as I was with him, I felt a sudden pang of sympathy for Eddie. "Where does that leave us?"

"Just with my instinct. Eddie is going home to think today, and come back tomorrow." He reached into the middle drawer of his desk and took out a salmon-colored three-by-five card. "In the meantime, I thought you might like another locker. This is the combination for a vacant one just down the…"

Terry shook his head.

"Why not?" I asked.

"It makes one of us look guilty of something. But nobody will know which one."

Rosen nodded, slowly. "I'm reassigning both of you, so people can't make assumptions."

"But they will," Terry insisted. "I want to talk to Eddie tomorrow, just him and me."

"I can't insist that Eddie talk to you," Rosen said.

"Did he want a new locker?" Terry asked.

"I can't discuss that," Rosen said.

"Can you wait until they talk?" I asked.

Rosen frowned.

"I don't need in my locker today," Terry said. "It's only my history book I don't have. I'll say I left it home."

The Twain Does Meet

I felt for Terry. He hadn't been in Ocean Alley but a few months. And he was at an age where his friends' opinions were the most important thing about school. Life, maybe.

Rosen looked from me to Terry. "If Eddie and you talk tomorrow, before school, then you two can come in here to see me for a minute. We'll decide then." He stood.

Terry picked up his backpack from the floor. "I can live with that."

We thanked Rosen and nodded to Mrs. Klinger as we left the office. Terry preceded me so he could hold the door to the hall for me.

The split second he was alone in the hall was enough for a mocking voice to ask, "Spent your money yet, O'Brien?"

I appeared behind Terry and opened my mouth to retort, but Terry's eyes told me not to.

Two boys about Terry's age saw me and froze as they stood at their lockers. The taller one reddened and the shorter one, perhaps Hispanic with very thick black hair, looked almost comical, holding a book in mid-air as he stopped its progress toward a locker shelf.

In an even tone, Terry said, "Tyler, Miguel, have you met my sister-in-law, Jolie Gentil?"

Tyler said, "Uh, nice to meet you."

Miguel added, "Good morning."

I wasn't about to say I was glad to meet them, so I simply nodded and said, "Good morning to you, too."

Terry met my gaze, and it kind of looked as if he was trying not to laugh. He pointed down the hall, toward the exit. We said nothing as we walked.

When we reached the security guard, Terry said, "I'll be right back in, Mr. Evans."

He boomed, "Didn't have that baby yet?"

I forced a smile. "I'm still counting the days."

When the door to the school shut behind us and we were on the sidewalk near the parking lot, I stopped and faced Terry. "How could you be so calm?"

He grinned. "Because you looked like you wanted to lunge at them, so I thought one of us should stay cool." He resumed walking.

"You are so damn like your brother."

"Thank you." He opened the car door for me, "You think it went okay?"

I heaved myself behind the steering wheel. "Maybe better than okay." I tugged on my seatbelt. "I thought your idea about the locker was good."

"Probably won't work. I don't see Eddie taking back his claim that I took the money."

I put the key in the ignition so I could put the window down, and looked at Terry through the now-closed car door. "You mean he'll have to save face?"

Terry shrugged. "I guess so. I think his mom and dad looked pretty mad."

I didn't get that. "He says he was the victim here. Unless they know where he got the money and aren't happy about that, why would they be mad?"

"Maybe they didn't know he had it. If he even did." He backed away. "I should be home on time."

"See you then." I started the car and watched his back until Terry entered the school. *How did he get so darn level-headed?*

I knew the answer. Losing his mom when he was nine was tough, though a married couple about her age, as opposed to Terence O'Brien's much older years, had helped a lot with the transition.

I snapped my fingers. Terry's photo album. I opened my phone. Though we didn't really stay in touch with them, the phone numbers for the couple who helped Terry were in my contact list. Frank and Linda Booker, in Florida. I sat for thirty seconds, mentally composing a note.

I decided on short and sweet. "Linda. We've been hunting for a photo album Terry thinks he had. Did he by any chance leave it at your place? Hope you're getting into spring."

Lame. I pressed send and put the phone in my purse. I didn't want a long response with a bunch of questions about Terry.

I thought some more. Terry had been lucky in so many ways. When Terence found out his death would be sooner rather than later, he brought Terry, to us. To Scoobie, really. Terry faced a lot of sadness, but he always knew there were people around who wanted to take care of him. Even so, he has a strong self-sufficient streak.

Self-sufficient or not, I knew Scoobie would want to know how the meeting went. I kept the car in park and thought for several seconds before I texted. "Rosen was reasonable. Instinct says Terry didn't take $$. Terry is OK. See you later." I did a smile emoji. *I could use a good laugh.*

CHAPTER SIX

I HAD WORKED UP an appetite after the meeting with Terry and Rosen. I thought about Java Jolt, which has bagels, but opted for Burger King, which was closer.

Burger King sat smack in the middle of downtown Ocean Alley, across from the Sandpiper Bar and not far from the First Presbyterian's Harvest for All and City Hall. Lester sometimes used Burger King to meet clients, but I decided to risk running into him.

I was a block from BK when I saw a hunched figure in a bright yellow hoodie a couple hundred feet ahead of me, walking quickly. Eddie Matlock. I couldn't say why, but something didn't seem right.

I pulled over a bit ahead of him, and brought the automatic window down. "Eddie. Is that you?"

He almost jumped from the sidewalk onto the stretch of sandy soil between it and the street. His startled face showed tears. "Yeah, uh, I gotta go, Mrs. O'Brien."

"Please, Eddie. I'll buy you breakfast. I'm heading to Burger King." He slowed slightly, and I added, "You don't need to talk to me about anything."

He stopped.

"Nobody's mad at you." Not totally true, but it seemed the right thing to say.

He turned to face me, and I noticed one cheek was bright red. Someone had slapped him.

"Everybody's mad at me!"

"I'm not. Please, Eddie, get in. We'll figure it out."

He frowned, and appeared puzzled. "Why would you help me?"

I smiled. "Because Scoobie and I used to get in trouble sometimes." *Nothing like what's going on with you.* Our behavior landed me in detention once. Scoobie spent a fair bit of time there.

Eddie hesitated, so I popped the automatic door locks. "Come on. Is Burger King okay?"

He straightened. "Yeah. Thanks." He opened the door and slid into the passenger seat. "I am kinda hungry."

After he fastened his seatbelt I pulled away from the curb. "I meant what I said. You're welcome to talk to me, but I won't ask you a thing."

He stared out the passenger window and said nothing, but it didn't seem like a sullen silence. I pulled into the Burger King parking lot.

We opened our car doors and I half-grunted as I got out.

"Oh, Mrs. O'Brien, do you need any help?"

"No, no." I faced him across the car's roof as I shut the driver's side door. "After the babies come I'll probably need a lot of help."

I clapped my hand to my mouth.

His eyes widened. "More than one?"

"Oh my God, Eddie. We just found out. I've only told immediate family."

A slow smile crossed his face. "I'm the first one besides them to know?"

I took my hand away from my mouth. "Please don't tell anyone else. I need time to…know what to say."

His smile vanished, and he nodded, solemnly.

I pointed toward the Burger King entrance. "Come on. You have to decide what you want."

Eddie moved to the door and opened it. "I think I only have a dollar."

Not quite the amount you mentioned yesterday. "That's okay. My treat."

We stood in front of the cash register and stared at the breakfast menu on the wall behind it. The cashier regarded us and occasionally shifted her weight from foot to foot. "You know what you want?"

"Um," Eddie said.

"Why don't you get a sausage and egg meal?" I looked at the cashier. "Comes with a drink right?"

"Yep. And breakfast potatoes."

"Okay, that's good," Eddie said.

"Let's see, I'll have an egg sandwich, no sausage. And milk, not coffee."

Eddie looked at me as if I had a sausage on my head.

I shrugged. "I have to eat healthy." I paid for the food and nodded toward the tables. "You can bring the food when it's ready. I need to sit."

The woman behind us in line held a two-year old, and she smiled at me. I moved away to sink into the hard plastic booth, and raised my swollen ankle to a spot on the booth bench beside me. I noted that Eddie stayed near the cash register, but he didn't move at all. Most kids pace or grab straws or something. He stayed still.

There were few enough people that the cashier didn't call the number on our receipt, which I had neglected to give to Eddie. She simply slid the tray across the counter toward him. Before coming to me, he took the plastic cup and filled it with some sort of soda and grabbed straws and a few napkins.

He slid in across from me and I took my eggs sandwich and milk, and grabbed a napkin. "I'm starved."

Without smiling, he began to unwrap his sausage and egg sandwich. "Me, too."

I inspected my egg sandwich and took a bite. Without enthusiasm I said, "Yum."

"You want some of my breakfast potatoes?"

I plucked two from his carton. "Real food."

We ate in silence for almost a minute before he asked, "Really, only Scoobie and Terry know?"

"And my aunt and uncle. I just found out yesterday. I didn't even stop at the hospital to tell Scoobie right away, because I didn't want him to faint at work."

That brought a grin. "You're funny." He swallowed. "And nice. No wonder Terry likes you so much."

I reddened slightly. "We're lucky he came into our lives."

"He told me his mom and dad died." Eddie fiddled with his sandwich. "But he mostly seems happy."

"He and Scoobie really hit it off. And I think my cat likes him better than me."

"Jazz," he said.

I realized Terry must have been friendlier with Eddie than I imagined. "Yeah, the little traitor."

Eddie smiled again, and then his eyes filled. "I'm really sorry."

I leaned back in the booth, awkwardly, since my leg was on the bench. "I bet things can work out."

"Terry will hate me." He blew his nose into a napkin.

"Terry...gets people. He didn't let Mr. Rosen assign him to a different locker, because he figured you two would...I don't know...get to the bottom of whatever it is."

Though he didn't smile, Eddie's entire expression changed. "So Terry doesn't want a different locker?"

I nodded.

"Can I come by your house after school? I know where you live."

"Sure. But maybe not before four."

He nodded and crammed the last of his egg and sausage sandwich into his mouth.

"Do, uh, you want your parents to come?"

He touched his left cheek in what seemed to be an unconscious gesture. "My dad says I'm a liar and I'm on my own."

One of the twins gave an extra kick. "I'm sorry things are...difficult for you."

He shrugged. "My mom's okay."

From near the entrance a male voice called, "Jolie Gentil as I live and breathe." George Winters stood there in his traditional garb of Hawaiian shirt and, in deference to his current job as an insurance investigator, khaki pants rather than cargo shorts. "Don't leave."

I gave George my four-fingered wave as I muttered, "Oh, boy."

Eddie regarded George's back as he turned to talk to the cashier. "He came to the soccer matches a couple of times."

"Yep. He's Scoobie's best friend."

Eddie balled up his trash. "I gotta go."

"You'll be okay until four?" Eleven or twelve did not seem old enough to roam the streets, though I supposed he could have been going home. I doubted it.

"Yep." Eddie slid out of the booth and headed for the door. He'd left me his trash on the tray with my barely-touched food. I ate a few more bites before George joined me.

"Kinda young for you, isn't he?" George asked.

"Terry's locker mate."

"Isn't it a school day?"

"He took off for a family thing. We ran into each other outside. What are you up to?"

George studied me. "You look weird."

I raised one eyebrow and stared at him. "You're the expert."

He grunted as he unwrapped the first of two egg-and-sausage biscuits.

"I'm just tired. What are you up to?"

"You already asked me that," George said.

I raised my arms in a shrug. "And yet, you didn't answer." I didn't really care what George was doing today. I wanted the conversation to be about anything other than my pregnancy. Scoobie clearly had not told him about our added cargo.

He slurped a glass of juice and spoke more softly than usual. "The company has me looking into an accident they think may have been caused by someone who was driving after he took sleep meds."

"Your insured or theirs?" I didn't really care.

"Theirs of course. They don't usually pay me to investigate ours. If I can prove it, they can maybe go after the other company to pay more of our client's medical bills." He started to drink more juice but stopped. "You aren't going to throw up again, are you?"

"I haven't done that since my fourth month."

"Well, you look…" he began.

Diversion tactic. "How do you drive after you take sleep medicine?"

"You don't do it intentionally. So I'm told. Some of the meds make you think you're awake, but you function kind of like you're in a trance."

"So, hide the car keys when you take sleep medicine?"

George talked for almost a full minute, the gist of which was you'd have to have someone else hide them, or your brain might know where to look for the keys.

I stifled a yawn.

"You heading home to take one of your naps?"

"I wish. I'm driving by the cape cod next to the B&B to help me think about what we should offer. I want to be realistic, but not too high."

"You definitely want it then? Seems kinda big."

Not anymore. "You know what a big plus the location is."

George grinned. "Aunt Madge gonna help you burp the baby?"

I finished my carton of milk. "You never know. She's getting older. We could be helping her and Harry more."

"Nah. She never ages. That baby'll make you ancient before she gets old."

CHAPTER SEVEN

I DROVE TO STEELE APPRAISALS, a.k.a Harry's former home, whose first floor is our office. Harry bought the small Victorian house because it belonged to his grandparents and he had fond memories of his summers in Ocean Alley. He put a lot of work into restoring it – refinished floors, a new porch, and a lot of paint -- but it still wouldn't be called pristine. I'm not sure why he hangs onto it. Probably because it would take a lot more time to finish fixing it up to sell.

I needed to check for new requests from local banks. Harry still worked the business, but as he has gotten more involved in the B&B with Aunt Madge, I'm usually the one who visits banks and realtors to drum up business. I've been lax the last couple of months.

I figured I had another month to work consistently. Then, even if I wanted to tromp around houses and yards, people might not want a huge pregnant woman poking around with a tape measure. They'd probably be afraid my water would break in their dining room.

The front door squeaked as I opened it, and I made a mental note to tell Harry to oil the hinges. I took in the staircase straight ahead of me. Harry wasn't doing too much remodeling up there now.

Though I always feel safe, I still glanced to the left of the foyer, into the huge living room, which ran almost the length of the house. I turned right into our office, with its two desks, work tables, and varied office equipment. In the back was the large kitchen, which led onto a back porch. Pre-pregnancy I would have headed there to make coffee. Decaf just doesn't seem worth it.

Such a shame to have the place empty most of the time.

Harry had been in recently. His desk had been decluttered and his in-box cleared out. My desk held two manila folders that hadn't been there three days ago. I scanned the contents, verified with the banks that we could do the work, and called both homeowners to arrange times to stop by.

I would do one tomorrow – a large house on the north end of town near Ocean Grove, and one the day after. The latter was a small cottage in a part of town we call the Popsicle District. Years ago someone had painted their bungalow a vibrant chartreuse, and since then all new paint jobs had been bright hues.

With a slight pang of guilt, I felt glad not to

have an appraisal today. I needed a nap. I also needed make a casual visit to the bank to make sure they had what they needed for our loan -- assuming Aunt Madge's neighbors accepted our offer. No pressure. Maybe I'd wait until tomorrow for the bank.

After checking at the office, I stopped by Java Jolt, to convey our surprising news. Megan took it in stride, with a comment that she thought I looked too big for one baby. Plus she gave me a caffeine-free latte on the house.

"You know, Jolie, two kids are manageable, but two infants will take all your energy. Will your sister and her girls help?"

"Renée will, and the girls are excited about cousins. I'm not sure Renée and Andrew have told them it's twins. I talked to them last night, after the girls went to bed." My ten and eight year old nieces, Julia and Michelle, say they can't wait to play with their new cousins, but I figure it won't be long until they're into boys and toddlers won't look so fun.

"You and Scoobie will be great." Megan smiled. "Plus, you'll be allowed to drink caffeine."

"Funny. You think your Alicia would babysit?"

Megan shrugged. "She might at some point, but your twins would have to be past true infancy. Two at once, when they're really little, would be too much for a teenager."

"You're right. I'm trying to think about too

many things at once."

I left Java Jolt and headed for the Purple Cow Office Supply Store. As I walked in, Ramona stood next to the cash register, cleaning a glass-topped counter with Windex. Her usual air of tranquility evaporated when I gave her the news.

She studied me for several seconds, open-mouthed. "Are you okay? Can you manage? Have you told Scoobie?"

"Yes to all. It'll be a lot different than we thought, but we have weeks to plan."

She nodded so vigorously that a few strands of her long, blonde hair escaped her French braid. "And you two will have Aunt Madge. And Harry."

"And my sister." I grinned. "And I hope not too much of my mother."

Ramona rolled her eyes. She'd met my parents only twice, enough to know she wouldn't want my mother's volume of free advice and to deem my father a saint. "Florida is a good distance. Plus, you'll have me sometimes, too."

I gave her a quick hug. Because I didn't want the conversation to stay focused on the babies, still a nerve-wracking topic, I told her about Terry's odd experience with Eddie and his locker. Ramona is a cultivated font of local information, but we have an agreement that anything I tell her about Terry is off limits for gossip.

She listened and frowned slightly as I finished.

"Is his father Malcolm Matlock?"

"I think so, unless there are two men with the same name. Why?"

"He has a solo accounting firm." She hesitated. "He used to be with a local firm, but he was kind of hard to work with, so they asked him to leave. Quietly."

"Huh. I don't really know them. I think," my turn to hesitate, "that either he or Eddie's mom may have slapped Eddie in the face. After they left the school this morning."

"Oh my." Chimes above the store's door tinkled, and Ramona nodded at a customer. Quietly, she said, "Don't leave."

I walked over to the stationery aisle to see the baby announcements the store stocked.

Ramona's manager called to me from the back of the store. "Jolie."

"Roland. Nice to see you."

He grinned broadly. "So, we'll have a little Jolie and a little Scoobie?"

I flushed. "Wow, where did you hear?"

"My wife just called. It's all over the hospital."

I put a hand on a shelf. "I'm so glad I came here early." R*amona would never have forgiven me if she heard about the twins from Roland.*

Roland's eyes widened. "You need a chair?"

"No, no. After the shock we had yesterday, nothing fazes me." Not true, but it made him relax.

"We're making an offer on a bigger house. A cape cod."

"Oh, right. Madge was in here the other day and she said she hoped you'd be able to get the place next to the B&B."

"And now I'm even more glad." I nodded at the shelf I stood next to. "Do you have birth announcements for twins?"

Roland became all business and explained that he could easily order them.

Behind us, I heard Ramona finish with a customer. She walked over.

"Did Jolie tell you?" she asked.

Roland had the good sense not to tell her he'd heard from his wife before he saw me. "Great news. You want to take a break, Ramona?"

She shook her head. "Jolie has a long list of errands. We'll just chat for a minute."

We walked toward the front of the store. "I do?"

She smiled, tightly. "I'll be quick."

We moved to a white board propped on an easel by the front entrance. Ramona writes a saying on it each day. On still days like today, it sits on the sidewalk. She picked up a dark green marker to finish writing. "Keep Calm and Carry On."

I decided I should repeat the phrase ten times a day for a while.

"Malcolm Matlock was so rude to me one time

that Roland came out to suggest he should speak more politely."

"Gee. What did he say?"

Ramona shrugged. "I don't remember exact words. The gist was that if I wasn't smart enough to work faster he'd go to Walmart."

I felt slightly sick to my stomach, not just from my morning sandwich. "Pretty nasty for Ocean Alley."

"He apologized, and he's been back. But you can see him stiffen if you don't do what he wants when he wants it." She leaned closer. "And I heard he keeps his wife on a really strict budget."

Maybe it makes sense that Eddie keeps money in his locker.

CHAPTER EIGHT

BEFORE GOING HOME, I stopped at the hardware store to get masking tape and a slew of packing boxes. We had planned to put our house on the market and move when it sold.

We'd have to reverse the order. We'd leave a few items in it so it would show well, but I didn't want to dawdle about moving. The last thing I wanted was to have to move after we had the babies. Babies!

I had checked out and headed toward the door when Sergeant Morehouse came through the automatic doors. With his close-cropped hair and polyester suits, he looked like he'd be a rigid guy. He isn't, but he doesn't like me looking into things he thinks should be left to the police. We hadn't butted heads in a while, not since before Scoobie's and my New Year's Eve wedding.

"Jolie. Good to see you." He eyed the flattened boxes in my cart. "Scoobie with you?"

"Nope. He's at work."

"I'll put 'em in your car." He reached for the

boxes.

"Thanks. My tax dollars at work."

"Don't push it." But he smiled.

"I hear Terry and Kevin hope to play on the same soccer team this spring. You think they'll both make the cut?"

Morehouse shrugged. "They look good to me, but I was a baseball guy. I'm not a good judge."

As I popped the button to open the trunk, I tried a question for Morehouse. "Did you hear Terry's locker mate accused him of taking some money?"

"Yeah, but I also heard there was no reason to think that's true."

"I think it will get resolved pretty quickly, in Terry's favor. But I thought Eddie Matlock's father seemed to be an...overbearing kind of man."

Morehouse lifted the trunk, placed the boxes in it, and turned to face me. "We aren't minding Mr. Matlock's business, are we?"

I shook my head. "Just trying to figure out the situation. Ramona mentioned..."

Morehouse looked skyward and back to me.

"That he was pretty rude to her in the store. And," I debated mentioning Eddie's red cheek, but decided to plow ahead. "I saw Eddie after the meeting at school. He had a bright red spot on his face."

Morehouse shut the trunk. "You talk to him?"

"Yes. He didn't say anyone slapped him, just that everyone was mad at him, and his father called him a liar and said he was on his own."

He frowned. "Can't say the attitude surprises me, and I'm sorry if he slapped his son. But if it was a frustrated parent acting inappropriately, and it's rare, it's not police business."

I wanted to tell him it was, but figured he knew his boundaries. When I glanced at him, I caught a smile.

"Are you going to tell me you never had even a tiny spanking?"

"Once, when I gave Reneé's doll a bath in the toilet, but never a slap."

He nodded, serious again.

"So, nothing to know about Mr. Matlock?"

He pointed a finger at me. "Jolie, you gotta let the boys work it out." He pointed at my stomach. "Ain't you got enough to deal with?"

I TALKED TO SCOOBIE at lunchtime, and we decided Terry was probably not going to have a major problem, but it was hard to see how things would work out. Before I could tell him about my conversation with Eddie, the Radiology receptionist buzzed him to say they had a walk-in patient.

I bought a few groceries, napped, and paced the living room a few times waiting for Terry to get home from school. Jazz watched me for a while, then curled into a ball on her placemat on the end table.

Terry came through the front door with a noncommittal hello. "We gotta talk."

"I'm all ears."

He dumped his backpack on the floor by the front door. "I'm hungry. You want anything?"

I leaned into the couch and fluffed my hair. "Iced tea would be good." *But I'd rather talk first.*

"Sure." Terry headed to the kitchen and opened the fridge before calling to me. "Thanks again for this morning."

"No problem." I ran my fingers through my hair again. I'd really flattened it when I napped. *How do I tell him I talked to Eddie?*

He came back to the living room. "It's fixed."

I took the tea. "Fixed?"

Terry sat in the rocker. "Eddie came by school this afternoon and Mr. Rosen called me to the office during seventh period."

"And that's good?"

"Yep. Eddie said he had money missing but there really wasn't a reason to think I took it. He said he was just mad and didn't want to get in trouble with his parents because it was gone."

I thought of Eddie's red cheek. "His dad?"

"I didn't really get that part." Terry frowned. "I think he already told Mr. Rosen something, because he said we should shake on it. I think Eddie might have to do an in-house detention for a day for lying, but he seemed okay about it."

"Did, uh, Eddie apologize?"

"Yeah, and the bell rang so we went back to the locker. I got my history book. I need it for some homework tonight."

"So that's it? Did those guys bother you anymore?"

"Your hair is messy."

"Check yourself in the mirror."

He smiled. "No, and Eddie and I kind of horsed around, so people could tell it was okay now."

A short beep from outside announced that Scoobie had just locked his car. He ran lightly up the steps and walked in quickly. He stopped when he saw me with tea and Terry lounging in the rocker. "Everything okay?"

I nodded at Terry. "You tell him."

Scoobie took a sip of my tea and sat next to me while Terry repeated what he'd told me.

"So," Terry finished, "I still don't know if he had money or any got stolen, but no one will think I took it."

Scoobie nodded slowly. "Something's going on in that home."

"I think so, too." I looked at Terry. "Does Eddie ever say anything about his parents mistreating him?"

"His dad sounds strict, but I've never heard anything specific, like they hit him or anything." His face brightened. "Scoobie, I made Mr. Rosen laugh."

When Scoobie heard my potty break story, they spent almost a minute reminding each other of times they'd seen me rush to the bathroom or burp during my pregnancy. Scoobie would never have said things like this on his own, but he knows how to play into a middle school boy's sense of humor.

"Uh, I meant to tell you." I swallowed. "I saw Eddie on the street, and treated him to breakfast at Burger King."

Terry's mouth fell open, and Scoobie stiffened.

"I wasn't keeping it a secret. There was just so much else."

Terry shut his mouth, but his expression had become very still. Then he said, "What did you guys talk about?"

"Nothing really. I saw him from behind, on the street, and something looked...wrong."

Terry reddened. "Well, yeah, he accused me of being a thief."

"Terry," Scoobie said, softly.

Both babies seemed to kick in tandem. "I know it seems odd. I pulled up next to him and said he didn't need to talk to me. I asked him to come to BK with me. He said he really was hungry."

Terry stayed quiet.

Scoobie opened his mouth to say something, but I didn't let him. "Remember when Mr. Rosen asked you if you could tell Scoobie and me anything?"

Terry nodded slowly.

"I didn't get the sense that Eddie can do that at home. In fact." I stopped.

"What fact?" Terry asked.

"One of his cheeks was red. Just one."

"Someone hit him?" Scoobie asked. "Maybe we should go get him."

Terry looked almost more shocked than when I said I'd had breakfast with Eddie.

I knew where Scoobie was coming from. His father was long gone when I met him in high school, and his mother had been mean. He didn't talk a lot about it, but I knew enough to feel certain he wished he could have gotten away from home. Maybe a lot.

I nodded to Terry. "Do you see indications that someone maybe slaps or hits him?"

Terry's shoulders relaxed. "I don't...think so. We're in phys ed together. Once he had a bruise above his elbow, but he said he was horsing around and fell out of bed and landed on his arm."

Scoobie rubbed his temple for a minute, not a usual gesture. He looked at me. "We have to be a little careful. If he isn't usually mistreated, a family services investigation would be a real hard thing for his family to go through."

"Okay," Terry said, and Scoobie and I turned to him. "I decided I'm not mad, Jolie."

Scoobie's lips twitched, and I said, "Good."

"But I'll sort of keep an eye on...I don't know...stuff. If he looks like someone's hurt him, I'll call Scoobie."

"Hey," I said.

For the first time, Terry smiled. "You'll be up to your elbows in diapers and baby poop."

CHAPTER NINE

I GOT UP EARLY THE NEXT MORNING. Early for me these days. Scoobie had left for work an hour earlier, and I was still in my bathrobe when I waved Terry off to school.

Last night we went over our proposed offer for the D Street house next to the Cozy Corner. If I know one thing about Ocean Alley it's property values. We made a fair offer and I couldn't think of a reason the owners would not accept it. But their opinion was the one that counted.

After a breakfast of plain yogurt and fresh strawberries, I headed for Lester's second-floor office in the small commercial building two blocks from the ocean, near Burger King. I tightened my sweater jacket as I trudged up the wooden exterior steps of the frame building. Plastered to the side of the yellow exterior walls were large plastic depictions of two starfish and a crab. Lester's landlord seemed to think these represented the best of the Jersey shore.

I figured Lester would not be in his office before nine. He often showed homes or met with sellers in the evening. Sometimes he'd read an appraisal Harry or I did, dislike the value we determined, and fire off an insulting fax at midnight. He always addressed the rude comments to Harry, even if I did the work.

Lester's default position was always to "offer more to be sure you get the house." Which of course would translate to a higher commission for him. That's why Lester's clients' offers and the appraisals we gave to the banks that were considering financing the mortgages sometimes differed.

As the real estate agent representing Scoobie and me as we searched for a house, Lester had been unfailingly polite. He had not followed what Harry calls his 'highball offer practices.' I suppose he figured that Scoobie and I knew enough to propose a realistic price. And he doesn't like to argue with me.

As expected, no Lester yet. I slid the signed offer under the door and returned to my car to head to the Second National Bank of Ocean Alley. We had submitted a mountain of paperwork to get preapproved for a loan. I wanted the bank to know they should be prepared to provide a loan sooner rather than the later time we had anticipated.

Everything needed to move quickly so we had

the chance to settle on the house before the hospital could make any layoff decisions. The thought of Scoobie's potential unemployment always made my stomach clench, which would be followed by baby kicks. No way to tell if one twin objected more than the other.

For some people, a meeting at a bank would be stressful. Since banks are Harry's and my clients, I knew almost all of the local branch employees. Even so, Mr. Gavin's question caught me off-guard.

"Is your husband's job going to get caught up in any potential layoffs at the hospital?"

I swallowed and forced a smile. "Everyone has been made aware of the possibility, but Scoobie hasn't heard anything to make him think he'll need to find another job."

Gavin nodded, his usual quick up-and-down motion. "Good. Because your own income fluctuates, his needs to be secure."

With that happy thought swirling, I headed for Harvest for All. I couldn't always do it, but I tried to be there for the first hour each of the three days we were open. Volunteers are pretty good about restocking shelves or letting me know what we're running low on, but I wanted to stay on top of it. At least for another month.

I arrived by nine-thirty for our ten AM opening, and was disappointed to hear a voice mail apology from a woman whose child had to stay home from school because of a fever. "Drat." I called her back and thanked her for telling me, saying I had other volunteers to call. Except I didn't, on such short notice.

Knowing I'd be working alone for a while sent me into high gear. Harvest for All is set up like a dry cleaner's except that instead of rolling tiers of clothes behind the counter we have shelves of food.

I finished checking the shelves for holes and restocked beans, oatmeal, and flour. We are fortunate to have a limited stock of fresh food and dairy items, thanks to a bequest from a generous friend, which let us buy some refrigeration units. It's more of a challenge to keep those foods in stock than beans or cereal.

Through the front window I could see a woman outside leaning against the glass, back to the pantry. Only ten minutes until we opened, but the fifty-five degree temperature could be chilly when you're standing still. I unlocked the door and motioned her in.

No doubt Mrs. Matlock could see the surprise on my face.

"Good morning, Mrs. O'Brien." She glanced at my nametag as I came in. "Or Ms. Gentil. Perhaps you aren't married to your baby's father?"

How rude. The occasionally snarky part of my brain immediately told myself that at least my additional pounds were baby weight. The polite part, always influenced by Aunt Madge, said, "Scoobie and I are married. I liked my maiden name."

At about five-two, Mrs. Matlock stood several inches shorter than I. As I walked behind the counter, she straightened to her full height and said, "I'm not sure which of our children to believe about Eddie's money."

I nodded as I faced her. "I can see this would be hard for you. We have also found Eddie's initial accusation...difficult."

"My husband is very angry."

I remembered the stiff Mr. Matlock leaving the school office. "At Eddie or Terry?"

Her composure cracked slightly. "He believes if our son had that kind of money he should have known about it. And that Eddie should have been more careful with it."

I didn't understand why Mrs. Matlock had come, and our patrons would soon arrive. "Does Eddie need to keep any money he makes in his locker?" Not that Terry knew of Eddie having after-school jobs of any sort. Those are hard to find for pre-teens, except babysitting or dog walking.

Her shoulders sagged somewhat. "Mr. Matlock is very thrifty. He regulates all our finances."

Who calls their husband Mister?"

I took a leap. "Do you feel you get enough for household expenses from your thrifty husband?"

Her eyebrows shot up and her face flushed. "I am also very careful with money."

"A skill I wish I'd mastered better." I smiled.

Her expression relaxed. "I simply came by to see if you had any idea where our...Eddie's money went."

I shook my head and paraphrased Mr. Rosen. "These he-said-she-said situations are a challenge, aren't they? One thing I'm sure of, our Terry would never steal."

"But how would you know?"

I took her tone to be earnest rather than offensive. "I guess I would pay attention to whether he, anyone, had spent an unusual amount of money. Maybe, I don't know, some special clothes, one of those computer game consoles." I did a sort of exaggerated shrug.

Mrs. Matlock stared over my shoulder for a second. "I should be going."

I gestured behind me. "Would you like a sample bag?"

I thought she was about to say yes, but the chimes above the door to the street tinkled, and a man carrying a toddler entered.

"Most definitely not." Mrs. Matlock turned abruptly and left.

That woman needs food.

CHAPTER TEN

I GOT TO THE LARGE colonial home twenty minutes past the appointed time. When the fifty-something homeowner opened the door, his scowl told me he planned to complain. Then he took in my baby bump (more like a baby boulder now).

He gestured I should enter. "Damn, young lady. You still have to work?"

As I walked into the foyer of the center hall colonial, I wanted to tell him pregnant women had been tilling fields for thousands of years, but decided he was simply saying he wasn't comfortable with someone so pregnant in his house. "I don't like to be bored."

He held out a beefy hand and I took it. "Victor Cribb. Lived here twenty-five years, mortgage is paid off and we're heading west. Won't miss the hurricane season a bit."

I looked up the stairs and thought they would be a bear to climb several times a day. "I doubt any Jersey shore person would." I smiled. "I generally go through the house and measure each room, then take some pictures for the appraisal report we give to the bank."

He led me to the entry to the living room and turned to face me. "Are you bonded?"

"Steele Appraisals is, which means I am."

He frowned. "I don't know this Harry Steele."

"Harry summered here with his grandparents as a child, and came back after he retired. He bought their old house."

"Married?"

I grinned. "He is now. To my aunt, Madge Rich…"

Cribb snapped his fingers. "That's how I know the name Jolie Gentil. Well, if you're Madge's niece, I'll go back to my coffee and let you wander around."

Yet again, Aunt Madge's sterling reputation had helped me.

I measured each room, noting closets, windows and doors – and carefully recorded the info. Every time I bent over, I felt as if I'd gained five or ten pounds in the last three days. Unlikely, but that didn't make me feel less ungainly.

I lumbered up the long staircase and took in the several doorways that faced the hallway. Two closets, a bathroom, and three bedrooms. In every room I tried to imagine how to arrange the furniture to accommodate two cribs. Wait, there would be at least one changing table, too.

This will just take longer if you let your mind wander.

It took me half-an-hour to finish my work inside and wish Victor Cribb well in his future home. Ten minutes to take exterior pictures and an hour to prepare the appraisal report. I felt as if I'd accomplished something and laughed at myself as I locked the door to Steele Appraisals. A few months ago the work would have been one of ten things I'd do in a morning.

WHEN TERRY CAME HOME from school, I was ready with a plate of banana slices and brownies. I hoped his day had gone as he expected it to.

He dropped his backpack and eyed the plate on the coffee table. "Is Aunt Madge giving you lessons?"

I thought he was being a smart-aleck until he grinned. "I always give you a snack, or leave one."

"Yeah, but you're always, like, mostly healthy about it."

"True. How was your day?"

He snatched two brownies, put them on a napkin, and sat in the rocker across from me. Jazz jumped off her favorite spot on the end table and went over to inspect his food. "It went okay. Eddie and I don't usually hang out, but we sat together at lunch."

"So, Eddie didn't have to do an in-house detention?"

"Not today." He chewed for a moment. "Mr. Rosen said he'd have to do a full day of in-house detention tomorrow. And Eddie has to explain why he brought the money to school and promise not to bring that much again."

"And that's it?"

"I guess." Terry shrugged, and then frowned. "I think I know where some of his money went. If it wasn't stolen."

That got my attention. "Where?"

"He's never had a phone before. Today he had one in the back of his locker shelf. I don't think I was supposed to see it."

"You're allowed to have them if you keep them in your locker, right?"

"Yeah, but he never has money. Now he has a smart phone."

"Does he do any, I don't know, jobs for people? Like raking leaves?"

Terry tilted his head, thinking. "He walks his neighbor's dog after school every day. I guess the man could pay him."

My brain shifted to a list of options. Maybe he had money and spent it, and didn't want to admit it. But if the money was his, who would care? Or maybe he took it from someone, or borrowed it and was supposed to give it back? Instead, he bought a phone.

"Jolie?" Terry sounded worried.

"Sorry, my mind wandered. I'm fine."

Terry studied the brownie in his hand. "A lot of kids at school have phones."

I tried not to smile. "You have your allowance."

"True...but when the babies come, maybe I should have a phone. You know, if you're out, and I need to call you, and the house phone is broken." He pointed a finger at me. "You know it's a good idea."

"I do, do I? You and Scoobie and I will have to talk about it. Do you have a lot of homework?"

"How come you ask me that whenever you don't want to talk about something?"

"It gives me a chance to think. In this case, also to talk to Scoobie."

He rolled his eyes. "I gotta get my soccer ball and shoes for practice." He jumped up to touch the ceiling light fixture near the front door as he moved to his room.

I stared out the window for a moment. Terry's pretty good about not playing Scoobie and me against each other, but when I saw Scoobie's car pull up, I figured I'd nip any possibility in the bud.

Terry raced for the door, and I called, "You can let Scoobie know you asked me about a phone, and

I said he and I would talk about it."

Terry did an exaggerated shrug and opened the door.

He and Scoobie fist-bumped and Terry said, "You and Jolie have a lot to talk about."

"You don't say." Scoobie raised an eyebrow in my direction, then nodded at Terry's shoes and ball near the door. "See you after practice."

"Yep, see you guys for dinner." He included both of us in his farewell and ran down the porch steps.

I raised my hands in a surrender motion as Scoobie bent to kiss me. "He wants a phone."

"Thought we might have a little more time before that came up."

"Maybe we can have him list why he needs it and how he'll be responsible for it."

Scoobie sat next to me. "That's very Aunt-Madge-ish of you."

"Renée suggested it. She said she figured he'd start asking pretty soon. Listen, I want to talk to you about Eddie's mom. She came to the food pantry today."

Scoobie frowned as he listened. "Kind of an odd conversation. You think she also wanted food?"

I nodded. "I'm pretty good at spotting folks who need it but don't want to say so. They kind of scan the shelves when they think you aren't looking. Act nervous."

"Huh. I don't see what more you can do than make the offer."

"True...oh, speaking of the Matlocks. Terry brought up the phone because Eddie seems to have one."

"Seems to?" Scoobie asked.

"Terry saw it just today, and he thinks Eddie meant to keep it hidden in the locker. Makes me wonder if that's where the money he might have had went."

Scoobie frowned. "His mom would have to have gotten it for him."

"Hmm. She might not know. You can get cheap phones and Wal-Mart and do month-to-month plans."

Scoobie shook his head. "Too much drama for my brain after work. And speaking of work."

"Uh, oh. What?"

"Rumor at the hospital is that any layoffs are going to be based on last-in-first-out."

I groaned. "And you were the most recent hire in Radiology?"

"You know I am. And Sam didn't say it. Like I said, a rumor."

I sank more into the couch. "We can manage, but it could mess up a loan application for the house." I told him what Mr. Gavin had said.

"Crud." Scoobie ate a piece of a banana from the plate on the coffee table. "Won't be for at least a few weeks. We should be okay if we can move fast on the house."

I dropped off our offer at Lester's office this morning.

Scoobie had an almost vacant expression for a moment. Then he stood. "I have to write something."

I left Scoobie to his poetry and headed to the kitchen to peel an onion and chop up a pepper to brown with the meat I'd use to make spaghetti sauce. I'd almost finished with the chopping when my cell phone rang. I answered without checking caller ID.

"Jolie? It's Mom."

One of the kids kicked a spot under my rib cage. "Mom. How are things in Florida?"

"Warming up, finally."

"You can send those forty-degree nights to Jersey anytime in February." Our usual meaningless banter.

She plowed ahead. "We of course can't wait to see the babies. But I thought you might want me up there to help before they're born. Maybe stay with Terry when you're at the hospital."

My brain did a mental shriek. "Gosh, that's so generous. Is Dad's ankle up to him being on his own?"

"Honey, he's on the golf course three times a week now. I usually stay with Renée, but you'll have the bigger house. I could stay with you and Scoobie."

The phone slid from my hand into the sink.

CHAPTER ELEVEN

AFTER TERRY WENT TO bed, Scoobie and I discussed my mother's proposition. I wanted the twins to know my parents, but the idea of having my mom in our house for an indeterminate amount of time made me bonkers.

"Could she be here some and at Renée's some?" he asked.

"I suppose. What I don't want is her giving Terry a lot of…advice. She gets so caught up in dressing a certain way or eating at the right restaurants. She'd badmouth Arnie's Diner and…"

Scoobie held up a hand. "We'll figure out a way to limit her time with us. Besides, she won't want to help with the move, so we don't have to deal with this for several weeks."

I sank further into the couch. "If I practice my baby breathing I can get my heart rate down."

He leaned over and kissed me. "The biggest reason I want those babies here is so I can get your heart rate up again."

THE NEXT MORNING I stopped by Steele Appraisals to see if Harry had reviewed the appraisal I'd done yesterday. I thought the pictures I took emphasized the house's strong points. He did too, and had no changes.

I made three copies, one for the homeowner, one for the bank, and one for Lester. I dropped a copy at the bank and two at Lester's real estate office.

After that, I headed for Harvest for All. Hopefully I would be there only long enough to check supplies and unlock the doors. Volunteers usually showed up on time.

After adding several items to the list of dairy products we needed to ask Mr. Markle to order, I was just leaving when Mrs. Matlock came through the door. The volunteers were busy with three customers, so I gestured that she should join me near the exit that led to the internal church hallway. "Good morning. Can I help you with something?"

She squared her shoulders. "It would be useful to sometimes get a few things."

I nodded. "That's fine. We can do that a couple of times without you registering with any of the social service organizations..."

She shook her head firmly. "We don't qualify for any assistance." She swallowed. "It's just that

Mr. Matlock believes we only need a certain amount of groceries."

I hesitated. Given that her husband had an accounting firm, her well-worn coat and older purse said something was amiss. We weren't unfeeling, but our resources were limited, and we tried to give food to the people who most needed it.

"We can do a few times, but..." an idea occurred to me. "You wouldn't be interested in a part-time job, would you? I'm going on maternity leave, and we've decided to pay someone for a short time."

"Instead of food?"

I shook my head. "We'd be happy to give you a bag today. I thought it would give you some...independent income."

She nodded, slowly. "I could say I'm volunteering. I'm allowed to do some volunteer work."

Allowed to do some volunteer work? I told her our hours and asked her if she could come in two days per week.

She squared her shoulders. "I can let you know."

Unsure what else to say, I gestured toward the counter. "Is there something specific you need, or should I fill a mixed bag?"

Mrs. Matlock followed me and stayed on the customer side of the counter while I moved behind it. "Peanut butter and jelly would be good. And do you have any rice?"

I added tuna, canned fruit and vegetables and soup, plus a small package of sugar and some oatmeal. I thought about how much food Terry ate and felt bad for Eddie.

I HEADED TO JAVA JOLT with thoughts of food pantry orders and Mrs. Matlock swirling in my head. The twins appeared concerned that I would forget them, because they kicked more than usual.

I patted the top of my twin bump. "Mama's right here. I think of you every minute." *Especially when you bump my bladder.*

When I entered Java Jolt, Megan greeted me with a cheery hello and pointed to a table close to the serving counter. "We haven't had a good chat in two weeks."

Max waved from the back of the shop where he was picking up dirty plates and rearranging chairs. "Jolie's here. Hi Jolie."

"Hello Max." I placed my shoulder bag on a table close to the counter and got myself a cup of decaf from the self-serve thermoses that Megan uses when it isn't tourist season. Then I argued with myself about the benefits of a cinnamon bun. I wasn't sure which choice meant I won.

The sugar bowl was almost empty, so I stepped behind the counter and scooped sugar from the canister she keeps on the employee side. Then I settled into my table to check my phone while Megan finished talking to people at a table in the back of the shop.

Megan slid into the chair next to me. "Are you feeling more even keel now that you've had a couple days to get used to the idea of twins?"

"Pretty much. We'll have to juggle a lot. I don't want Scoobie up a lot at night and then having to go to work."

She patted my hand. "You'll figure it out. And your sister will help."

I rolled my eyes. "My mother wants to stay with us for some period of time. I love her, but we butt heads a lot."

Megan grinned. "She might look better when she's changing a diaper at three AM. Any word from Sylvia on when she'll step in to do more?"

I shook my head. "She wanted at least a week to go over order lists and our volunteer book."

Megan arched an eyebrow.

I smiled. "I don't think she wants to get in the way of how you manage volunteers. She said she wanted to know how everything is done."

Megan did a 'whew' gesture across her brow.

"I have a question. Do you know the family of Terry's locker mate from school?" I described the Matlocks.

"Megan slowly shook her head. "I don't think

they're customers here. Unless they come in really rarely."

I became aware of Max standing very still, a few feet from us. "What's up, Max?"

"Mr. Malcolm Matlock? Not the Matlock from the TV show. TV show."

Megan gestured to the chair next her. "You know him?"

Max sat. He usually doesn't sit at one of the tables, so he gave the impression of expecting his seat to cave in or something. "Met him. Two times. Two. He came to the Veterans Outreach Center, but he didn't like to talk in our group. Our group."

I didn't know much about Max's interactions at the center. Scoobie or George occasionally drove him to meetings or counseling sessions because the center was at the edge of town, by the highway.

"Is he, um, someone you like?" I asked.

Max frowned. "He used to come there. We sat in a circle together. A circle."

Max was very aware of his eccentric speech patterns and simple logic. Most people were kind, but he could be exasperating if he got stuck on a point and asked a lot of questions.

Max looked at Megan. "He drank regular coffee. I think decaf would be better. Decaf."

Megan smiled. "Wound up kind of tight, is he?"

"Grouchy," Max said.

"Ah. Does he still come to the circles?" I asked.

Max shook his head, "He wanted everything to go fast. Fast."

I couldn't always infer Max's meaning, but this time I thought I could. "You mean like impatient?"

Max nodded. "You don't go to circles, Jolie, but you know Malcolm Matlock. Matlock."

"Yes. His son is Eddie, and he shares a locker with Terry. At the middle school."

Max's eyes brightened. "Scoobie's Terry. Terry."

"Yes."

Max stood. If you didn't know him, it would seem abrupt, almost rude. But when Max finished a conversation, he left it.

"Back to work. Work."

Megan pointed to the pastries that sat on a round stand, under glass. "You ready for a donut?"

"After I sweep. Sweep." He moved toward the back of the shop.

Megan met my eyes. "Is this Matlock man someone you've had a run-in with?"

"No, but I've seen his impatience. I wonder if he might take it out on his son."

"Not good. Is there a Mom?"

I snapped my fingers. "I mentioned to her that she might like to work a few hours a week at the pantry. It would give her some extra grocery money."

Megan frowned. "Would it bring an abusive

man into Harvest for All?"

"Gee, I didn't consider that. I'll keep my ears open, but I'm not sure I know anyone who would tell me anything."

The people in the back of the shop stood and began to put on jackets and pick up purses. Megan stood. "Okay. You going to train her?"

I nodded. "I'll work with her a couple of times."

I finished my decaf and left money in the sugar bowl Megan keeps next to the thermoses during the off season. I didn't think I'd be putting the pantry in any danger if we hired Mrs. Matlock. But how would I know?

RAMONA WAS ON THE PHONE when I entered the Purple Cow, but she ended the conversation quickly.

"I didn't mean to interrupt."

She fingered the bottom of her French braid, which hung over her shoulder. "You didn't. Just finished taking an order."

I didn't see notes on the pad in front of her, and decided she must have entered it directly into the small computer that provided inventory information and served as a cash register. "You have a minute?"

"Sure. Someone from Beachcomber's Alley is coming over to pick up a big batch of pens to keep behind the front desk. She said something about them walking off."

Ocean Alley's oldest hotel attracted only tourists in the summer, but in the winter and early spring, it hosted a lot of college students and a few small business conferences. "Did you personalize the pens?"

"Yep. What's up?"

I told her about my conversation with Megan and Max. "You said he was asked to leave the accounting firm he worked for so he started his own business. Did you ever hear he hit anyone, or anything like that?"

She shook her head, firmly. "Nothing like that."

Relief washed over me. "Good. Because we could use someone a few hours a week while I'm on maternity leave, and…"

Ramona laughed. "Listen to you. Reverend Jamison practically had to drag you onto the food pantry committee, and here you are talking about taking maternity leave from a volunteer position."

"Jeez. I need my head examined."

She grinned and pointed toward the door. "Go home and take a nap. You look tired."

CHAPTER TWELVE

WHEN I GOT HOME I studied my reflection in the bathroom mirror. Even my eyes looked exhausted. "If you think you're tired now, wait until the twins come."

I lay down on the couch and put its decorative pillow under my head. Jazz saw this as an opportunity to nap, and hopped onto my chest. I stared into her green eyes. "You realize I don't have any kind of lap, right?"

She yawned and drew herself into a tight ball. I stroked her head. "I hope you can adapt to babies as well as you adapted to Pebbles."

A sniff came from the floor near the couch. I glanced down at Pebbles. "You know you don't come up here."

She raised her tail and turned away. It doesn't matter how many times she does that, for a second I forget she's had her scent glands removed.

MY CELL PHONE RANG at ten after two. I jerked awake and fished in the pocket of my maternity top. "Hello."

"Jolie? It's Art Rosen. Sorry if I woke you."

"Occupational hazard in the third trimester. Is Terry okay?"

"Fine. But he thought Eddie moved pretty stiffly when they were at the locker this morning. Terry said you told him to come to me if he noticed anything amiss with Eddie. Did you have a specific reason for telling him that?"

"No, just a hunch. I saw how angry Mr. Matlock was when he and his wife left your office the other day."

"That's it?"

"Oh, and Eddie's cheek looked red to me when I saw him at Burger King later. If I had anything more than that I'd have talked to you. Did something happen?"

"I wouldn't normally discuss this with someone besides Eddie and his parents, but Terry did come in. He said that in PE Eddie left his long-sleeved t-shirt on instead of changing into gym clothes. It made him think Eddie was hurt. Long story short, I asked the nurse to call Eddie to her office. He has a large bruise on the side of his rib cage."

I gasped and sat up. Jazz meowed loudly and jumped to the floor. "My God."

He sighed. "I don't know Malcolm and Agnes Matlock well. I've talked to Eddie. He insists he fell off his bed, and he's angry at Terry for talking to me."

"That's...maybe not good."

"But common sometimes, in cases like this. We have a protocol to follow. Please don't discuss this with anyone else."

At the same time, Rosen and I said, "Except Scoobie." He hung up.

I placed the phone on my chest, lay against the pillow, and put my hands across the top of my tummy. The twins were apparently playing soccer. "Cut it out, you guys." I inhaled some deep breaths, and they took a time out.

I judged Matlock to be in his mid-forties. Maybe he was simply mean. Or maybe he served in Iraq or Afghanistan. Did he have PTSD? Was he keeping horrors bottled up and swinging at his son instead of getting help?

Terry would be home in an hour. I sat up and swung my legs onto the floor. This struck me as definitely a day for a fresh batch of brownies.

THE FRONT DOOR SLAMMED as I took the pan of brownies from the oven. "I'm in the kitchen, Terry."

His backpack hit the floor with a thud and he stormed into the kitchen. "Do you know what Eddie said to me? All I was trying to do was help him."

"I don't know what he said, but Mr. Rosen called to say you talked to him and the nurse talked to Eddie."

Terry tossed his bangs to one side. "Mr. Rosen called you?"

I sat the brownie pan on a cooling rack. "Yes. He seems to think you did the right thing."

He slid into one of the two chairs at the small kitchen table. "He could hardly turn sideways."

I sat across from him. "I'll cut you a brownie when they cool a little. Mr. Rosen more or less said he would handle it."

He fidgeted with the salt shaker. "Eddie said I made everything worse."

I put a hand over Terry's. "I don't think it's a situation Eddie can handle alone."

"What about his mom?"

We both listened to Scoobie's car pull into the gravel driveway. I nodded at Terry. "Why don't you bring him up to speed and then the three of us can talk about it in the living room."

Terry hurried onto the porch and Jazz meowed. I glanced down at Pebbles and Jazz sitting by the back door. "Okay, it's warm enough to go outside for a few minutes. Jazz, make sure Pebbles stays near the porch."

Terry rolled his eyes. "They don't speak English."

"She gets my tone." I opened the door and Jazz

scampered down the steps while Pebbles waddled behind her. I always worried that someone would think she was a wild skunk. Of course, if they called the animal control officer, he could tell them she was tame. The entire block knew her.

Scoobie came in the front door as Terry finished a recap of his day.

"Hello, Preggo," Scoobie called.

"Keep it up and I give Pebbles your brownie."

"As long as you clean up the mess later."

Terry laughed. A good sound.

Scoobie came into the kitchen as I began to cut the brownies. He kissed my cheek. "We'll get settled in the living room. Can I bring anything in?"

"You can take the napkins. I only have one plate." I finished cutting the brownies, two for the guys, one for me. I felt really full.

When I walked into the living room, Terry started to get up from a spot next to Scoobie on the sofa, but I gestured that he should stay there. I sat on the rocker and placed the plate on the coffee table. "Help yourselves."

No one said anything while we each grabbed a brownie. Terry took a bite and closed his eyes. "These are so good. Is this Aunt Madge's recipe?"

"Get real," I said. "It's an eighty-nine cent box from the dollar store."

Scoobie grinned, then grew serious. "I've explained to Terry that we have to help people sometimes even if they think they don't want it."

Terry leaned back into the sofa. "Eddie called me a rat. But not too loud."

I sighed. "The school system will know how to reach out to his parents."

"I kinda think it's his dad. He always says his mom packs him a good lunch."

Scoobie and I smiled at each other. Scoobie stood. "We can support him, but we can't fix it for him. Why don't I drive you and Kevin to the big practice field at the high school?"

Terry crammed the rest of his brownie in his mouth and jumped up. "I'll get my ball."

I did a palms up shrug to Scoobie and spoke quietly and quickly. "Max says Eddie's dad is a vet, but got impatient in a group at the Outreach Center."

Scoobie glanced toward Terry's room. "One of the guys in the blood lab said Matlock was in Afghanistan for a tour."

Terry bounded back into the room. "I'm ready."

"It'll take me thirty seconds to get out of my scrubs."

After they left, I let Jazz and Pebbles in and sat on the couch with a notepad. I wanted Eddie to get help, but I knew if I obsessed on it the babies would tense. At least that's how I thought of it when they seemed to settle in a harder lump near the bottom of my tummy.

I started making a list of supplies we had to buy immediately. We wouldn't have bouncing babies in the next few days. It was too early. I wrote quickly. Diapers, bibs, baby powder, diaper ointment. "Jeez. Where will we put all this?"

AFTER DINNER, TERRY SAT AT the desk in his bedroom while Scoobie stretched out on the couch with a book. I had the newest Stephanie Plum book, but couldn't get lost in it. I sensed Scoobie's gaze on me and looked up. "What?"

"Rosen will work with the right people to make sure he's safe."

I smiled. "Could you have imagined yourself saying that when you were in high school?"

"Nah." He lowered his voice. "One time I told him if he wanted to chill out I knew where he could get some good weed."

I put my hand over my mouth to stifle a giggle. "You never told me that before."

"You were too straight. Plus, Aunt Madge would've killed..."

The phone interrupted him. Scoobie stood. "I almost forget we have that land line phone." He walked to a small table on the far side of the room.

I half-listened to his part of the conversation, but Terry stuck his head around the door jamb. "If that's for me, I could've answered it on a cell phone and you guys wouldn't have had to bother."

I pointed at him. "Finish your geography."

He pulled his head back into his room. "I could also do research on it."

Scoobie frowned as he hung up the phone. "Who was that?"

"Guy from work, wants to trade a shift." He sat down on the couch and picked up his book.

I whispered. "It was not."

He nodded his head toward Terry's room. In a low tone he said, "In a minute."

My heart pounded and I felt an acid taste in my throat. "Damn heartburn."

Scoobie's eyes brightened and he spoke in a normal voice. "Heartburn? I could get you some Tums."

"I can just sip some water..."

He winked at me and raised his voice. "Terry, I'm going to the drug store to get Jolie some Tums."

He called back. "Too much burping?"

I rolled my eyes. "Or not enough." I widened my eyes so Scoobie could tell I wanted to know where he was really going.

He bent next to me. "That was Matlock mouthing off. I want to talk to someone at the station. Maybe one of the guys we know'll be on duty and they can give him a friendly call."

My eyebrows arched. "Is he dangerous?"

Scoobie shook his head. "When I told him I'd buy him a milkshake at Arnie's Diner he got quiet.

Then he said 'never mind,' and hung up."

I stood and walked him to the door. "You're sure it's okay?"

"Yeah, bullies like him are all talk."

Except with their kids.

From his room, Terry called, "I can hear you whispering."

SCOOBIE CAME BACK IN forty minutes. He'd even remembered to stop at the drug store. He tossed me the small bag of antacids. "Terry, you winding down?"

Terry came out of his room. "Yeah. My geography's done, and I started my math, but it's not due until day after tomorrow."

"Change your clothes and brush your teeth and I'll finish beating you in that chess game."

"I'm not five," Terry grumbled, but he grinned and went back into his room.

Scoobie watched me wrestle with the child proof wrapping on the Tums jar and took it. He sat next to me and spoke quietly. "It's all good. When he's asleep, we can talk."

I listened to them comment on each other's moves. I could always tell when they were close to the end of a game because they stopped kidding around. I tried to focus on my book, but my chin kept hitting my chest. In a haze, I heard Terry say, "Goodnight, sleepy head."

That roused me and I blew him a kiss. I closed the book and stretched. I wanted to be awake when Scoobie thought it was a good time to talk.

Our lives were so different than a year ago. It's not like we were regular party goers or anything, but our time certainly didn't revolve around a kid's school schedule and sleep needs. Good practice, probably. Pretty soon it would be diapers and sleep deprivation.

After twenty minutes, Scoobie closed his book and peeked into Terry's room. He pulled the door almost shut. "Out like a light."

I patted the spot next to me on the sofa. "What happened?"

"The jerk started off telling me we should take care of our kid and he'd take care of his. I told him I got that, but our kid didn't get punched in the ribs at home."

"What did he say?"

"Told me to mind my effing business. That's when I offered to buy him the milkshake. He mumbled 'never mind,' and hung up"

"Okay, so what happened at the station?"

"I got lucky. Morehouse was finishing his shift late. Said he had a dentist appointment this morning. He'd already talked to Rosen. Said it's tough, because Eddie's old enough to talk for himself and he insists he fell."

"You told Morehouse what Mr. Matlock said?"

"Yeah, he thinks he's a windbag, but a windbag with a problem too big to ignore."

"No kidding."

Scoobie smiled grimly. "So we called Matlock together."

"How'd that go?"

"He was more polite to Morehouse, but he insisted anything that went on in his house was nobody's business. Finally, Morehouse said he didn't want to make it a police matter. He said if Matlock would go to the VA Outreach Center with him tomorrow and get set up with a counselor, that would be a first step to calming down. I think that's how he put it."

"That seems kind of, I don't know, informal."

Scoobie nodded. "Apparently there're a few people, men, I think, who've had recent deployments and have what Morehouse called a short fuse. The center here is pretty good, so the police work with them to try to address things before they get to be criminal matters."

I frowned. "I think if you hit a kid it's criminal."

"Everybody does. But if there's a way to address it without arresting him -- especially because it might be hard to prove -- Morehouse wants to go that way." Scoobie shrugged. "He hates to see a veteran in jail instead of in some sort of treatment."

"So now what?"

"Morehouse is picking Matlock up at nine to go to the center."

"And then what?"

Scoobie shrugged again. "We may never know exactly what. If it goes well, anyway."

"I hate not knowing."

He grinned. "I know you do." He sobered. "I trust Morehouse. And I guess he'll talk to Rosen."

I didn't say anything, just fiddled with the couch pillow.

"You know, one of these days we'll be dropping the kids with a babysitter, or having one here. You'll have to learn to trust."

"Yes, but we'll still be more or less in charge."

Scoobie tugged my hair. "I think when those kiddos come we won't be in charge of anything for years."

I frowned. "Every time we talk about the future, I worry about your job."

"You remember worrying doesn't change anything, right?"

"It makes me feel like I'm doing something."

Scoobie held up crossed fingers. "I heard it's getting less likely that Radiology will lose a position. At least not before Labor Day. Have to be able to take care of the tourists when they break bones."

"So I should move it down a notch on my worry list?"

Scoobie did an exaggerated sigh. "Haven't I taught you anything about living one day at a time?"

CHAPTER THIRTEEN

SYLVIA PARRETT AND I MET at Harvest for All the next morning to go over a list of questions she'd prepared. She'd done a lot for the pantry, but she'd never been involved in day-to-day operations such as managing the inventory or coordinating with social services agencies who sent some of our clients to us.

I gulped when I saw a page-and-a-half of questions. Thankfully, most of them were easy to answer. "A bunch of these are sort of 'it depends.'" I smiled at her raised eyebrows. "I know you like precision, but we don't always have a lot of that."

She nodded. "Megan said I can call her for advice."

"She knows as much as I do. And within a week or so after the kids come, you can call me."

"I'm the last person you'll want to hear from."

"No, that'll be a crying baby at three AM."

Sylvia smiled. "You just take care of yourself."

"You can work with me for a while. Watch

what I do and it'll give you a feel for actually distributing the food."

"I won't be in here a lot..."

The front door banged and we both looked toward it.

Mrs. Matlock barged into the pantry. Her red face and pointing finger said a lot about her mood. "You need to stop paying attention to my son!"

Sylvia stepped back, and I put a hand on her arm. "It's okay. I know her, and this isn't food pantry business." To Mrs. Matlock, I said, "Come into the hall with me."

Sylvia's look of alarm seemed to have calmed Mrs. Matlock somewhat. She said nothing, but nodded at Sylvia and followed me into the church hallway.

I faced her. "We don't want to mind your business, but Eddie seemed to be hurt. That's not something to ignore."

Her face reddened again. "I can handle it."

I tried to keep derision from my tone. "You knew he was hurt and sent him to school."

She lifted her chin. "We went to the urgent care place yesterday evening. They x-rayed him. He's got a bruise, but his ribs aren't hurt bad."

"I'm glad to hear that, but how do you know it won't happen again?"

The fight seemed to go out of her. "You, you don't understand. Malcolm is a good man. It's just sometimes he gets, he doesn't know how to handle, he isn't sure what..."

"Perhaps you mean he can't manage his anger."

She straightened her shoulders. "He hasn't always been this way. Only since he came back from that last deployment."

I knew she was probably torn between helping her husband and protecting her son, but I couldn't grasp why she didn't put Eddie first.

"You don't understand," she began.

"Maybe I do. Or I know how Scoobie grew up."

She frowned. "What do you mean?"

"Scoobie's dad had PTSD, too. He simply left the family."

Mrs. Matlock looked away. I wondered if she sometimes wished her husband would do the same. "But the problem was, he left Scoobie with an alcoholic mother who wasn't always good to him. He had a tough time."

She stiffened. "I'm sorry to hear that."

"My point is, he was a kid, he was scared. You don't want Eddie to be scared in his own home."

Her eyes filled with tears. "And I don't want some police officer taking my husband to jail either. He, he doesn't mean it. He, he..."

"He needs help," I said, gently. "Didn't Sergeant Morehouse pick him up this morning, to take him to the Veterans Outreach Center?"

She almost shuddered. "He didn't want to go."

"I get that, but they can help him. He isn't alone."

"I don't want him to be even angrier when he comes back."

"Do you have family here? Maybe someone you and Eddie could stay with for a few weeks, just until he talks to counselors or something?"

She shook her head. "My brother and his family are in Oregon. If it were winter, some cottages are empty. I've thought about talking to a family I know who close up for the winter, but it's spring."

I snapped my fingers. "I might have an idea. Let me make a phone call." I pointed to a grouping of chairs at the end of the hall. "Have a seat while I call someone."

Harry was empathetic, but he wasn't sure he liked the idea of people he didn't know living in his upstairs.

Aunt Madge got on the phone. "We don't have many guests until mid-May. Maybe they could stay here for a couple of weeks and we could get to know them. Is she with you?"

"Yes. Hang on." I took my cell phone to Mrs. Matlock. "You know the Cozy Corner B&B?"

"On D Street? Of course."

"My aunt owns it. She wants to talk to you."

In five minutes, we had the outline of a plan. Mrs. Matlock would stop by the B&B to meet Aunt

Madge and Harry. When Mr. Matlock got home, she would suggest that they talk about some time to reduce tension in the house by having her and Eddie stay with Aunt Madge and Harry for a few days.

Mrs. Matlock handed me my phone. "Now that I know we have an option, I'll be strong enough to insist it's a good plan. I felt so...hopeless before."

"And maybe after he talks to people at the VA Center he'll be more receptive."

We walked back into the food pantry. "Are you still interested in working here a few hours a couple of days a week?"

Sylvia had been reading a folder as she stood at the counter. She looked up, and I read caution on her face.

"Sylvia, this is Agnes Matlock. She's had a rough couple of days, but she feels better. She's going to try working here a few hours a week, that idea we discussed at the last meeting."

To her credit, Sylvia relaxed and offered to show her the ropes.

BY THE END OF THE three hours of serving customers, I was wiped out. Sylvia had stayed to watch how I did things, and Mrs. Matlock ended up being a big help. She caught on quickly to how the food was organized and I was able to sit at the counter while she grabbed a lot of the items for our clients.

I needed a nap, but before I went home I drove to the boardwalk and climbed the steps. The temperature was a mild sixty degrees, but the wind was from the ocean, so it was chilly. I leaned against a railing and stared at the waves.

By sometime in late spring, Scoobie and I would be wrestling a stroller up the steps and pushing babies along the brightly colored stores. Terry would be a big help, but a lot would be on me, especially the first few months when I'd handle most of the feeding.

I wanted to appreciate the peace and quiet while I had it. A gull landed on the railing a few feet from me and bobbed its head. "Sorry pal, no food." He squawked and hopped onto the sand below and pecked at something.

From behind me, a man called, "Hey, Jolie."

I turned. George Winters, notebook under his arm, came toward me. "What are you doing?"

"Just enjoying the breeze."

He nodded toward Java Jolt. "I'm heading down there to drink coffee and work up an insurance estimate. Wanna join me?"

I shook my head. "I'm going home to nap."

He leaned on the rail next to me and stared at the water. "Scoobie told me about that kid at Terry's school. And that his old man called your house."

"He did. I just talked to his wife. I think there's a plan to help the family."

"That's a lot for you to have to worry about right now."

I smiled. "Aunt Madge and Harry are helping."

He laughed. "Well, there you go. Scoobie said Morehouse was going to talk to the guy."

"Yes, sort of informally. So maybe Eddie's dad can get some help from the VA or someplace."

"Yeah, Scoob said the guy's a vet. Those guys saw a lot of bad stuff." He pushed back from the railing. "Gotta run. Good of you guys to look out for the kid." He loped toward Java Jolt.

I pulled my sweater tighter and shivered. I needed that nap.

WHEN I WOKE UP on the couch at two-thirty, Jazz was on my chest, her nose three inches from mine. "How long have you been there?"

She placed a paw on my cheek, then drew it back.

"Thank you for the pat. It's going to get kind of noisy around here. Well, at our new place. Assuming we get it. Think of all the places we've lived the last few years."

She meowed. "I know, you miss Mister Rogers and Miss Piggy. Maybe you can visit for a couple of days when the babies come."

My cell phone rang and Jazz hopped to the

floor. I sat up and dug in my purse, answering it on the fourth ring. "Hello."

Lester spoke at top volume. "Jolie. Good news. They accepted your offer. You guys got the house."

CHAPTER FOURTEEN

I GOT UP THE NEXT morning already knowing there wouldn't be enough hours in the day. After dinner last night, Scoobie and I drew up to-do lists for the next two weeks. The sellers had already moved a lot of their stuff into storage so they could show the house, and their retirement home was ready and waiting for them in Florida.

My hope was that even if it took a few weeks for the loan to go through we'd be able to rent the new house so we could get our furniture in with time to spare. And then we had to get our house ready to sell!

I patted my baby bump. "Calm down you two."

I shifted in the rocking chair and took a sip of coffee. I felt out of sorts. Not mentally, just kind of like something was off. For a moment I wondered if I should worry about the babies coming early. Scoobie and I had talked about it a little, and Renée had warned me to pack a bag to be ready to go to the hospital.

The Twain Does Meet

Aloud I said, "I don't have time to deliver you two now." And I didn't. I planned to go to the Popsicle District to appraise a small cottage. It shouldn't take long, and I debated as to whether I could do the measurements myself. I wasn't about to kneel on the floor.

I stood and walked to the kitchen to put my coffee cup in the sink. Time to get to work. I grabbed my purse and a sweater from the coat closet. Good thing the weather was getting warmer. I certainly didn't have any coats that fit anymore.

The two-bedroom cottage sat on a tiny lot, one of many carved from land that surrounded the spacious homes that dotted Ocean Alley long ago. It still had its original clapboard exterior, though the bright blue paint and white trim were new.

I dropped the key as I entered and made an oomphing sound as I picked it up. In less than twenty minutes I finished taking measurements and snapping interior photos before heading outside.

As I stood on the sidewalk trying for a good angle to take a picture of the front of the house, a car pulled up to the curb at the next house. I didn't pay much attention until a man called, "Ms. Gentil?"

Because he pronounced it Gentle, I knew it was not anyone I knew well. I turned and almost dropped my camera as Malcolm Matlock approached me. At six feet and wearing a somber expression, Mr. Matlock scared me.

He took in my startled face and raised his hands, palms toward me. "Sorry, I didn't mean to concern you." He stayed about ten yards away.

I took a deep breath. "Okay. What, uh, are you up to?"

"I was driving to work. I wouldn't have noticed you, but you are pretty pregnant."

I smiled and he did the same. "Very much so. Twins."

"Eddie told us that. Listen," he looked at the house and back at me, "I'm sorry I called your husband last night."

"Thanks. That makes me feel better. Hearing you say that, I mean."

"You and your husband, you could've made a big deal about that."

I nodded, unsure what to say.

"My wife and I talked. I guess you know the offer your aunt and uncle made."

It still felt funny to hear someone call Harry my uncle. Even after he and Aunt Made had been married two years. "I'm glad you like the idea. I mean, if you do."

He nodded, slowly. "I didn't at first, but Agnes is right. It will be easier. Just for a short time."

"Take the pressure off."

"And it's not like we're separating," he said, quickly.

"Of course." What else could I say?

He smiled again. "Madge said if Agnes and I want, I can come by for muffins in the mornings."

I grinned broadly. "She's a special person. You can meet her golden retrievers."

He gestured to his car, an older SUV. "I'll let you get back to work."

"I'm just about to finish up here and head to the office."

He gave an off-handed wave, got in his SUV, and drove off.

My shoulders relaxed. I'd only been afraid for an instant, but my heart still beat fast. "What a way to start the day."

I texted Scoobie. He hadn't been sure he liked the idea of Mrs. Matlock and Eddie at the B&B, so I wanted to tell him how positive Mr. Matlock's reaction had been.

I drove to the appraisal office, glad to have plenty of time to write up the report. I felt so tired. "You better get with it, Jolie, you have a busy few weeks coming up."

After finishing the report I stopped by the post office to pick up change-of-address forms and then stopped by Mr. Markle's store to make sure he'd heard we were having twins. I found him in the fresh produce area unloading a box of lettuce.

He placed the last head on the rack and wiped his hand on his broad, white apron. "Ramona stopped by yesterday and told me the news. Does that new house you're getting have all the bedrooms on the main floor?"

I laughed. "The ones that count. Terry and the guest room will be upstairs."

"You have everything organized at Harvest for All so you don't have to worry about things?"

"I'll probably still worry, but we have one new person and Sylvia's going to do some of my duties for a while."

He began to open a box of apples. "She knows where to find me if she needs a quick order."

BACK AT THE HOUSE I was soon asleep, awakened at two-thirty by someone on the front porch. When they didn't knock, I glanced out the door to see a large envelope on the step and the mail truck pulling away.

I opened the door and stepped onto the porch. "Great, more bending over." The sturdy envelope had been sent from Florida. "Oh, my. Terry's pictures."

Should I open it? My name was on the label, but the photos were Terry's. Then I wondered if Linda Booker had put a note inside. A note for me. I knew she still hurt from not having been able to raise Terry. Not that his father had said she would.

I decided to open the envelope to check for a note, but not to open the album. The album was about twelve by twelve inches, and easily ten years old. Or maybe as old as Terry. Sitting on top of it was a lavender envelope addressed to me.

Dear Jolie,

We got your text. I should have mailed this months ago. Your request came at a good time. Frank and I just found out we're pregnant. A big surprise. We really didn't think it would happen again.

I'll leave it up to you about whether you tell Terry. He put a note in the birthday card he sent me. It sounds as if he's really busy. And happy. I'm glad it all worked out.

Linda Booker

Short and sweet. I'd forgotten Terry asked Scoobie to help him pick out a card for her. A few months ago I might have felt jealous. Now I was glad he had thought of her. Selfish of me, but I also felt relieved that she was pregnant. She had a miscarriage some time ago, and her husband thought that had been why she focused so much on Terry.

I stuck the letter in my purse. Scoobie and I would have to decide what to tell Terry.

I placed the album on the coffee table, then moved it to the small table by the television. I didn't want to be tempted to open it.

For the next forty-five minutes I had some energy, so I dusted, did a load of laundry, cleaned and washed some broccoli and carrots. Terry would be home soon. I hoped he would want to wait until Scoobie came home to look at the album, but I wouldn't insist he do that.

The front door opened at three-fifteen, and Terry came in calmly. Quite a contrast to yesterday. "Everything go okay at school?"

"Yeah. Did you bake brownies?"

"Nope, there a few left from yesterday. Eat an apple first."

He did an exaggerated shrug, pretending not to want to eat the apple. "Eddie's not mad. He's less stiff, and he said his dad was going to that VA Center this morning, so he'd feel better."

It didn't sound as if Eddie had told Terry about Scoobie and Sergeant Morehouse's role in arranging that. Probably a good thing. I hoped we would soon be far less involved in the Matlock family's lives.

I sat on the couch, exhausted after my not-so-extensive chores. "Come and tell me about your day."

Terry opened the fridge and poured himself a glass of milk. He came into the living room with the drink and his apple. "Nothing big. I got a good grade on my geography homework."

"Super. When Scoobie gets home, there's a surprise."

"What is it?"

"Is Scoobie home?"

Terry rolled his eyes and reached down to pet Pebbles, who had waddled to him. Jazz sat on her placemat on the end table. She always wanted the taller perch.

Scoobie's car pulled into the driveway and Terry opened the front door. The fresh air felt good.

"What's the surprise?" Terry called.

Scoobie came in and ruffled Terry's hair. "You need a haircut. What surprise?"

They both looked at me. "Check out the photo album on the other side of the room."

"Oh, wow." Terry bounded across the room and grabbed it. "There's a bunch of mom and dad in here, too."

He sat between us on the sofa and opened the album. The first thing I noticed was that the pictures of him at about age one showed him with both brown and blonde hair.

Scoobie pulled one from its page. "Son of a gun. That's me."

"Yeah, so?" Terry said.

I leaned over Terry to look at it with Scoobie. "We don't have any photos of Scoobie at that age."

He spoke softly. "My sweet mother threw them all away when she was mad at me one day."

Terry's eyes widened. "You're kidding."

Scoobie didn't respond.

I kissed the top of Terry's head. "I'm glad your dad kept them."

Terry took the photo from Scoobie. "I didn't see these until, I dunno, a year ago I guess." He looked at Scoobie. "Remember, he didn't tell me about you until…" His voice trailed off and he wiped a tear from the corner of his eye.

Scoobie pulled Terry to him in a hug, and our eyes met over the top of Terry's head. I mouthed, "Wow."

The brothers pulled apart. The album had slid to the floor and Terry picked it up. "Dad put pictures of you and me next to each other. There's maybe five or six. I guess that's all he had."

The pictures of Scoobie were from about age one to eight. My eyes glistened. "We'll be able to compare your baby pictures to the twins."

Scoobie picked up a photo of him at about age three, holding a stuffed bear. "I was a handsome dude, wasn't I?"

Terry moved to the next page. "I smiled more."

"Yes," Scoobie said. "You did."

Scoobie and I locked eyes for a moment. I said. "I think our twins will smile a lot, too."

Terry looked up. "You're going to have to start calling them more than just 'the twins.'"

"We've got ages to decide on names," I said.

CHAPTER FIFTEEN

WE'D HAD AN EMOTIONALLY draining day. A good one, but draining. When Scoobie suggested crib shopping for after dinner, it sounded almost relaxing.

A Babies R Us store used to be a couple of miles from Ocean Alley, but it closed when the franchise went out of business. That left us with the local Walmart or a trip to a mall several miles away. We opted for Walmart.

Terry talked almost incessantly about all the things we needed to buy. He also wanted to know when he would be able to give the babies a bath and whether it would be okay that he saw our little girl "without her clothes."

"You take that one," I muttered to Scoobie.

He glanced at Terry in the rear view window. "It's fine for babies. They can't do anything for themselves, so we need to help them with everything."

Terry started to ask something, but Scoobie

kept talking.

"Did everything get resolved about Eddie and his locker money?"

"Terry leaned forward. "I forgot. I know why he kept money there."

Together, Scoobie and I said, "Why?"

"He said his Dad like to have all the money, or kind of say where it all goes. And sometimes he and his mom like to buy other things."

I turned my head toward Terry, and Scoobie looked in the rear view mirror again.

Terry caught my eye. "So if Eddie makes some money, like walking the neighbor's dog, or maybe his mom does – but I don't know how – they keep it in his locker."

"I see," Scoobie said. "And do you think he lost some?"

"Well…I kinda think he spent some on his phone and he didn't want to tell his mom."

"Did he tell you that?" I asked.

"Nope, I just think it."

Scoobie pulled into a parking space in front of the store. "I guess that's between him and his mom."

"Yep." Terry opened his door and almost bounced toward the store. When he was about twenty yards ahead of us, I glanced up at Scoobie. "I don't see that we can really do anything more."

Scoobie laughed and took my hand. We don't often walk hand-in-hand these days because my gait is so awkward. "Gee, you must have some hormone issues. You want to butt out."

I kind of smirked at him. "Maybe I'm just tired."

Scoobie laughed, but before he could respond, Terry's voice drifted across the parking lot. "You two are so slow!"

Scoobie called back, "Jolie's slow. I'm being polite."

Terry laughed and half-jogged into the store.

I shook my head. "He knows we make the decisions on what to buy, right?"

"He asked me about soccer decals for the boy's bed. After I reminded him our girl could be on an Olympic soccer team, I also said the choice was ultimately yours, so we'd wait."

"Ours," I said, firmly.

"Yes, but…I'll be at work a lot, you'll be the one putting side rails up and down the most, or whatever we figure out we have to do with a crib."

"Okay. You can change the diaper pail the most."

He laughed. "As long as I can paint a few lines of poetry on the headboard…"

I dropped his hand and elbowed his arm. "No poetry until they can pick their own." I patted the arm I had just elbowed and we crossed the street in front of the store and entered.

Terry finished talking to a yellow-vested store

employee and came over. "I found out where cribs are. All the baby stuff." He turned, assuming we would follow him.

Scoobie called, "Hey Terry. Let's walk together."

Terry slowed and we caught up. He grinned. "Jolie walks slower than babies crawl."

We turned right at the end of the main aisle and I tuned into Terry's plea to Scoobie. "If we put them together now, it'll be all done."

"And put them where?" I asked.

Scoobie kept his expression impassive. "Terry's room, right?"

Terry stopped and faced us. "Oh, I guess we don't have space, do we?"

"Since we'll be moving into the new place before the babies arrive, the second day we're in the house you guys can assemble them."

"Not the first?" Terry asked.

"First day you'll have to get your own room organized," Scoobie said.

"Oh, yeah." Terry grinned. "I need to put some smelly socks under my bed."

I pointed. "I see cribs and rockers."

Terry moved ahead and Scoobie did a one-arm hug across my shoulders. "Thank you."

In a low, singsong voice, I said, "Thank me again and I won't make lasagna for months."

I stopped and pointed to the infant clothes,

which sat across from the children's furniture. "You start on the cribs. I want to look at some onesies and bibs."

"Your sister said after we moved she'd have a box of infant stuff, right? Oh, is it all pink?"

"Nope, a lot of yellow and green, too. I just want to buy a couple things myself." I grinned. "Besides. I hear twins can come early."

"Sheesh." Scoobie turned to follow Terry. "I guess we'll get gifts after they're born, too."

"Sure. My sister talked about a shower, but I told her I never know which days I'll have a lot of energy."

Over his shoulder, Scoobie said, "See you later, Preggo."

Fifteen minutes later, I had picked out a few items and Scoobie had jotted down some information about two of the cribs we'd seen. A clerk said we would have more choices online, and they could be delivered to the store. Or us.

Scoobie and Terry walked a few feet ahead of me with our bags, and Scoobie whispered in Terry's ear.

Terry stopped and stared at Scoobie, open-mouthed.

"Come on Numnuts," Scoobie said, and they kept walking.

I caught up. "I'll be ready for some hot tea when we get home. Who wants to make it?"

THE STREET IN FRONT OF OUR bungalow was more crowded with cars than usual.

"Somebody must be having a party," Terry said.

"Or a meeting," Scoobie said. "Sometimes Charlotte Evans has Rotary committees meet at her house."

We pulled into our narrow gravel driveway. Scoobie pointed to the porch. "Terry, why don't you head up first and put a cup of hot water in the microwave for Jolie's tea?"

Terry dashed up the steps and Scoobie came to the passenger side and opened my door. "At your service, m'Lady."

I giggled and grabbed his hand as I lifted myself out. "I swear, our duo sank to the bottom of my uterus today."

"Uh." He shut the car door. ""Is that a good thing?"

"Not good or bad. Just a load shift." I glanced at the front porch. "Did Terry bring his key?"

"He must have." Scoobie grinned. "I suppose any jokes about wide loads are off limits?"

I slapped his elbow, which was becoming a habit. "They always are. And never use such a term around George."

We climbed the steps and Scoobie said, loudly, "That's a promise."

He opened the screen door and then the main one, letting me walk ahead of him.

Flashes and laughter greeted me, followed by a roar of voices.

"Surprise!"

CHAPTER SIXTEEN

THE FIRST PERSON I took in was Terry. He stared around the room, open-mouthed. Then Ramona's face came into focus and I became aware of Scoobie's steadying grip on my elbow.

Ramona clapped her hands a couple of times. "We really got you, didn't we?"

My face must have been three shades of crimson. "I didn't even have an inkling." I turned to Scoobie. "No wonder Terry didn't need a key."

I spoke to Terry as I let my sister kiss my cheek and lead me to the rocker, which had been festooned in pink and blue ribbon. "You kept a good secret."

Terry shook his head. "Not for long. Scoobie said it got…what was it, Scoobie?"

He and George spoke together. "Moved up."

Renée laughed. "Twins sometimes come early."

I saw two card tables of beautifully wrapped packages in front of the window, but before I could say anything, Scoobie said. "What a haul, you guys."

George pointed a finger at him. "Convenient of you to be gone when we had to bring it in fast."

Scoobie affected a saintly demeanor. "I had an important job. Deceiving my wife." He pulled up a folding chair and sat on my left, while Renée sat on my right, ready to make notes about who gave what.

Aunt Madge brought me a cup of punch and ruffled my hair. "Sorry, not spiked."

I laughed. Today her hair was blue with a pink stripe. I blew her a kiss. "I'm light-headed already. You really got me."

Terry passed me the first gift. Each time we opened one it reinforced how many friends we had, and from so many parts of our lives.

Ramona attached a rattle to a handmade gift card for pen-and-ink baby drawings for the first three years of the twins' lives.

Morehouse and several other police officers bought a tricycle, and on the handlebars hung a sign saying two miles per hour. "We bought the thing for one kid, so they gotta share."

Scoobie called toward the kitchen. "Aunt Madge, get out of the kitchen."

She stuck her head around the corner. "You aren't the boss of me."

Terry whooped. She pointed at him and said,

"Last batch of muffins in the oven. I'll be right out."

Harry came out of the kitchen with a tray of muffins, some with pink frosting, some with blue. "I told her you'd want her out here."

George pulled open the back door. "Hot in here."

Our little house wasn't made for almost twenty-five people in its living-dining combo. I wondered where all the folding chairs came from.

Sylvia Parrett banged two spoons together. When she had almost everyone's attention, she held up a circular from Carter's baby store. "All of us at Harvest for All chipped in for a nice gift card."

"Thank you," Terry said. Several people laughed and he blushed.

"You're welcome." Sylvia actually smiled. "We have a suggestion. They have several strollers for twins. We want you to be able to walk to the food pantry."

"Real soon," Megan added.

Monica spoke up. "I'm learning to crochet so I can make booties."

I imagined one two inches longer than another, and mentally slapped myself.

Almost every gift reflected its giver. Daphne gave us a box of coated cardboard books, Mr. Markle a box of baby food, and one can of formula. Pinned to it was a note that said, "For your nights off." That brought a lot of laughs.

Every time I noticed Lester he was peering into a room or down the hallway. I called to him. "Lester. We'll give you lots of time to poke around before you list it."

Ramona rolled her eyes. This appeared to be one of those nights she felt embarrassed to claim Lester as her uncle.

I had just finished hugging Reverend Jamison so he could leave when I had a sensation that made me look toward the bathroom. *Drat, it's busy!*

I sort of lunged for the kitchen, heading for the back porch. I almost made it before my water broke and smelly liquid ran down my legs onto the tile floor.

George turned from the bowl of chips he had been refilling and yelled, "Get Scoobie."

Harry called, "Where's Madge?"

Renée beat them both. "And you don't call her sister?"

The next ten minutes passed fast. I sat on a kitchen chair, half embarrassed, half wanting to laugh hard. For Terry, who stood just outside the kitchen door, I stayed fully calm. Outwardly.

Scoobie mopped up the water and put the towels on the back porch. "You wanted an audience?" He grinned. "I'm going to say good-bye to folks for just a minute." He went into the living room.

Ramona came into the kitchen carrying a nylon

carry-all bag that usually hung on the bedroom closet doorknob. She held it open to show Renée, who grinned. "Looks good to me."

"What's that?" I asked.

Renée said, "The 'go bag' you hadn't packed yet. Nightgown, comb, toothbrush. All that stuff."

I peered into the bag. "I wish I could have a glass of wine."

"Soon enough," Aunt Madge said.

Suddenly, a sharp pain shot through my belly. I half expected to see a knife protruding from my navel. I leaned over. "Ooh-ee."

Terry called, "Scoobie!"

Harry put a hand on Terry's shoulder. "All normal. Come on, let's get your PJs so you can stay at the Cozy Corner tonight."

"Where are Jolie and Scoobie going?" Terry asked.

"The hospital. You may have a brother and sis...I mean nephew and niece when you get up tomorrow."

Scoobie knelt in front of me and spoke gently. "If your water hadn't broken I would've made you ride on the car roof."

My eyes filled. "Hurts. Maybe hurry."

Scoobie stared into my eyes. He didn't move his head. "George. Ambulance."

"What the..." George began.

Scoobie said, "Now."

Aunt Madge came back into the kitchen, took in the scene, and said, "Everyone out except Renée and Scoobie." She turned and began shooing anyone else into the living room.

From near the front door, Harry called, "See you guys later. You've got this, Jolie."

I don't feel like it.

"Do your breathing," Scoobie said.

I did a few short puffs, just as the pain began to wane. "I can't believe I forgot."

Scoobie put his forehead on mine. "That's why you have a coach."

Morehouse's voice came from the living room. "Show's over, folks. I'm sure Scoobie will let a couple people know the big news and you can pass it on."

Sweat beaded on my forehead as another wave of pain began.

"Breathe, baby." Scoobie looked up at Renée. "How long between?"

"Thirty seconds since the last one ended."

"Sheesh. Check to be sure George made that call."

From the kitchen doorway, Aunt Madge said, "I did it myself."

Scoobie smiled. "Better than a general calling the troops."

Through clenched teeth, I said, "Better, *gasp*, be. Where's Terry?"

Aunt Madge said, "Harry just hustled him out."

Tears ran down my cheeks. "Scoobie, it really hurts."

"I know. I'm sorry I can't fix it."

I gasped again, then groaned. "You got me into this fix."

"Indeed he did," Renée said.

I could hear the smile in her voice.

"I think it will all be done soon, Little Sister."

I became aware of red lights dancing on the front windows and heavy footsteps thunking up the porch.

Morehouse said, "Gotta hurry, guys, I think. Where's your gurney?"

"In the ambulance," a male voice said.

"Get the damn thing."

I didn't know how I was supposed to feel so soon after the onset of contractions, but everything seemed too fast. Much faster than what we were told in the classes we'd been taking.

Scoobie said, "I'm just moving a few inches so the paramedics can talk to you."

The gentle face of a huge black man said, "I'm Jerrod. We're going to get you to the hospital really fast. How far along are you?"

Another wave of pain hit me, and Renée said, "We think thirty-four weeks. It's twins."

In the blur of the next few minutes, Aunt

Madge handed me a dish towel "to chomp on" and the kitchen table was somehow replaced with a gurney.

The gentle giant and his short female partner – I thought she said her name was Gloria – kept telling me I'd be fine. They half-guided, half-lifted me onto the gurney.

I puffed as they strapped me onto the rock-hard transport. "I think…one is…close."

"We've got you," Gloria said.

They pushed me to the door, which Morehouse held open. "I'm lights and sirens ahead of you."

I wailed, "Scoobie."

"Right here, I'll be right next to you."

Gloria said, "I don't think…"

Morehouse said, "Does he have to miss it?"

"I work at the hospital," Scoobie said.

"He does," Aunt Madge shouted. "In radiology."

Gloria grunted as she and Jarrod lifted the gurney into the ambulance. "Okay, just stay out of the way."

A horn honked, and out the back door of the ambulance I saw George and Ramona in the front seat of his car. "Renée. Madge. Hurry up."

I heard running, then Scoobie and I were in the ambulance and sirens filled my ears. "Scoobie!"

"Hold my hand," he said.

I gripped it, and his fingers closed over mine, loosening them a bit. "We won't have to buy a vise." He grinned and ran his hand over the top of my head.

"It's coming," I yelled."

Calmly, Jerrod said, "Crowning."

Scoobie and Gloria said, "Big push."

"Take that curve slow," Jerrod called to the driver.

I bore down and pushed with all my strength. "Oooph. Ow!"

Gloria yelled, "You're doing great!"

I felt a bowling ball drop from me into Gloria's hands. Or I hoped she caught it.

Scoobie's face was in front of mine. "It's our boy. We have a boy!"

The ambulance stopped and its back door almost flew open. I was vaguely aware of a bunch of men and women in many colors of scrubs, most of them masked.

Dr. Madison's voice, calm as if she'd been in church, said, "Let's hear that first cry."

And our little guy cried and someone said something about cutting the cord. Then the gurney was out of the ambulance and being wheeled into the ER.

In a few second, I screamed, "She's coming."

Our parade stopped and Dr. Madison stooped in front of the gurney. "Push, Jolie. Help her,

Scoobie."

As I pushed I saw an incubator whiz by. So many lab coats and scrubs surrounded it, I couldn't even see Lance.

"Lance," I mumbled, and pushed as if everything depended on it.

▲

CHAPTER SEVENTEEN

I ROUSED FROM MY drowsy, pain-shot reveries. "Scoobie, did you see them yet?"

He stood from the plastic chair next to my bed in the delivery suite. "They said I could, but I thought I should wait until…"

"Are you nuts?" I grinned. "Give me a full report in a couple minutes."

"Love you." He slurped a kiss on my cheek and jogged out of the room.

A nurse spoke from across the room. "You sound much better. Won't be too long before you can head to the nursery, too."

"Thanks. It was a wonderful, blessed experience. Just so…" I really couldn't think of a word. Fast? Unexpected? Crazy? Painful?

I really wanted to see our babies, but Dr. Madison said the nurse needed to monitor my vitals for a while before I could. I got that. If you deliver a full-term baby in an orderly fashion, you hold the baby right away. If your kids appear prematurely in a chaotic scene, the babies need to be checked out. And so do you.

The nurse said I would ride to the nursery in a wheelchair. I didn't want to be so fuzzy I'd fall out of it.

I shut my eyes, but opened them when a soft voice said, "Jolie?"

"Dr. Madison. How are they?"

"In the capable hands of the neonatal pediatrician, who says they are pretty amazing." She patted me on the arm. "Their mom did a good job."

I took in the bars of my bed, and the balloon hanging above her. "You're delivering balloons now?"

She smiled. "Apparently a delegation of your friends wanted to see you two, but that's not going to happen tonight. What was the man's name...?"

"George Winters," I said "most likely."

"Yes, the former reporter. He said Sergeant Morehouse prevailed on the security staff to open the gift shop and you now have this balloon and the rather large card that's sitting by your feet."

"Oh, my."

"Scoobie may be with the twins a few more minutes. Would you like me to open it for you?"

"That seems above and beyond the call." In truth, I wasn't sure if everything on the card would be good clean fun, so to speak.

She tied the balloon to my bed rail and slit open the card.

Probably fifteen people had signed it.

Ramona: "Jazz will be jealous. Love you."

Sergeant Morehouse: "Talk about timing. You know how to pick it."

George: "I got a lot of good pictures."

Under that, Aunt Madge's handwriting said, "I have his camera."

I closed the card. "I don't want to deprive Scoobie of being the first to read these lines."

She patted me on the arm. "I'll stop in tomorrow morning, Jolie. You did great." Dr. Madison left.

The door swooshed and I glanced at it eagerly, expecting to see Scoobie. Instead, Aunt Madge, Renée, and Ramona entered.

Renée almost ran to me, leaned over, and put her cheek on mine for several seconds. "My baby sister is a mommy."

I kissed her cheek. "Faster than we thought, but it's all good. I told Scoobie to go see them. I have to wait a little longer."

Aunt Madge smiled broadly. "To think you and Jazz arrived in Ocean Alley alone, and now look at you."

I held out my arms, IV lines and all, and she gave me a gentle hug.

When she pulled back I did my best to give the three of them a kind of evil eye. "Who planned the shower?"

Renée said, "Ramona."

Ramona said, "Renée."

Aunt Madge laughed. "Both of them. It was supposed to be at the Cozy Corner in two weeks, but when we heard it was twins, that seemed too long to wait."

Ramona added, "And Scoobie said you were tired in the evening, so we thought we'd just pop in and out at your place."

"Good plan. Something sure popped out. Thank you so much. Such lovely gifts. I'd just started to buy things."

The door swooshed again and this time Scoobie came in. His face radiated happiness. "They're amazing." He leaned over and kissed me on the lips.

"We're heading out," Renée said. She blew him a kiss. "They let us come in because Scoobie left."

She bent over me, smiled, and whispered, "I know you delivered early so Mom and Dad would have to stay with me when she came up."

"Don't tell on me."

Renée and Ramona left.

Scoobie took in Aunt Madge. She held out her arms and he walked into them.

I saw my husband cry for the first time. Short,

gulping sobs.

Aunt Madge hugged him and patted him on the back. "You're making the life you always wanted, and you're doing a great job."

He pulled back, wiped the back of each hand over his eyes, and gave me a watery grin. "I can't believe so many things are coming together. And to think we used to sit under the boardwalk and aim through the cracks with squirt guns."

I reached for Scoobie's hand.

"No doubt your children will do the same." Aunt Madge leaned over to kiss me. "I'll head home to Harry and Terry. Harry already explained it's too late for Terry to come over tonight."

"We'll call him in a few minutes," Scoobie said, and I yawned and nodded.

Finally, we were alone again. Scoobie pushed a recliner next to my bed. "You did all the work, but I'm whipped."

"Tell me more about them."

He reached for my hand. "Very pink, not too wrinkled. Dr. Madison said because it was a fast birth." He frowned. "They have these tiny IVs, and little oxygen cannulas. That's kind of hard to see."

"Are they sleeping?"

He grinned. "Yeah, but when one of them moves, the other one wakes up, too. Then they go back to sleep."

"I'm getting impatient."

Scoobie glanced at the monitor device on a pole next to the bed. "Your numbers look good. I bet we can go together soon." He tilted his head. "Did I hear you call our boy Lance?"

"It popped into my head. What do you think?"

He nodded, slowly. "A strong name of a good friend."

Lance Wilson had died the past Christmas Eve, well into his nineties. He'd been Aunt Madge's friend for decades and, after I took over at Harvest for All, mine as well. His dry humor made hard things easier.

"So, we need a name for our lovely daughter," I said.

"Do you think her name needs to start with an L?"

We sounded out several names. Leslie, Laura, Linda, Lucy. None seemed perfect.

Scoobie's phone buzzed. He pulled it from his pocket and smiled at the caller ID. "The Cozy Corner. Aunt Madge must have said he could call." He pushed the answer button. "Hey, bro. You're coming tomorrow, right?"

He listened. "Just a minute." Scoobie covered the mouthpiece. "Should we tell him Lance's name?"

"Sure. He can tell Madge and Harry, but no one else." I closed my eyes. My stomach rumbled, and I decided that when Scoobie hung up, he could find my nurse to ask for a tray.

Meanwhile, I listened to Scoobie's end of the conversation, and gathered that Terry, Scoobie, and Aunt Madge had varied opinions on a name for our daughter.

Scoobie stayed noncommittal on a choice. "Terry, I need to pay attention to our main lady here." He listened. "You can stay home all day."

I smiled. "No school. That'll be the best part of all of it."

Scoobie stowed his phone. "He seems to like the name Leia, like Princess Leia in *Star Wars*. What do you think?"

"We could pronounce it like that, but I think I'd like to spell it L-E-A-H."

Could that confuse her?" Scoobie asked.

"She won't know any difference, and I think it's better than three vowels in a row."

"Speaking of vowels." Scoobie reached into his breast pocket and pulled out a folded piece of paper. "I've been working on a poem. I just finished the last line."

I will build for you a garden of love.
Then, in the evening,
When you walk through the garden alone,
The fragrance of our love will always linger there for you.

A garden, where the rustling leaves above hide the

birds
As they sing their soft notes of love.
A garden where the gathering clouds of evening
Will not hide the glow of happiness in our hearts.

A garden that does not need the gentle rainfall
To flourish the beams of joy and hope for all.
A garden where the gentle breeze
does not cool our ardor for you,
And it's always at your beck and call.

It's a garden of love for all.

My eyes filled. "Do you have a title?"

"To Our Children in their Pursuit of Happiness."

AFTER I ATE AN ENGLISH muffin and an apple, the nurse pronounced me fit enough to go down the hall to meet the twins. Scoobie assumed the role of wheelchair chauffer.

As he pushed me, I asked, "Could you tell which one was a boy and which a girl?"

"Not without the blue and pink caps on their heads. At least we'll always have a sure way to check."

I laughed. "My guess is pretty soon we'll be able to tell even when the diapers are on."

A nurse led us into the nursery, and I stepped out of the wheelchair to reach into each incubator to touch our children. Lance and Leah breathed softly.

Two new lives, created from two people who were lucky to find each other again.

Aunt Madge was right. I had more joy than I could have imagined a short time ago. We had happy lives ahead of us.

THE END

ABOUT THE AUTHOR

Elaine L. Orr primarily writes traditional or cozy mysteries – defined as mysteries without a lot of gore that feature an amateur sleuth. Her Jolie Gentil cozy mystery series has eleven books and a prequel, and now this novella. *Behind the Walls* was a finalist for the 2014 Chanticleer Mystery and Mayhem Awards. The first book in her Iowa River's Edge series, *From Newsprint to Footprints*, came out in late 2015, and the second book, was a Chanticleer finalist in 2017. The Logland series began with *Tip a Hat to Murder* in 2016. The newer series each have three books – so far.

She also writes plays and novellas, including the one-act play, *Common Ground* published in 2015. Her novella, *Biding Time*, was one of five finalists in the National Press Club's first fiction contest, in 1993. Her favorite book is the novella *Falling into Place*.

Elaine conducts presentations and book publishing and other writing-related topics. Nonfiction includes *Writing When Time is Scarce: and Getting the Work Published*.

Elaine grew up in Maryland and moved to the Midwest in 1994. She received her B.A. from the University of Dayton and M.A. from the American University. She did some journalism course work at the University of Maryland and took fiction courses from The Writer's Center in Bethesda, MD, the University of Iowa Summer Writing Festival, and Georgetown University's Continuing Education Program. Elaine is a regular attendee at Magna Cum Murder. She is a member of Sisters in Crime and the Indiana Writers' Center.

OTHER BOOKS
BY ELAINE L. ORR

Elaine's books are generally self-published, via Lifelong Dreams Publishing and are at all online retailers as ebooks, paperbacks, large print, and audio. Barnes and Noble can easily order paperbacks.

Jolie Gentil Cozy Mystery Series
Appraisal for Murder
Rekindling Motives
When the Carny Comes to Town
Any Port in a Storm
Trouble on the Doorstep
Behind the Walls
Vague Images
Ground to a Halt
Holidays in Ocean Alley
The Unexpected Resolution
Underground in Ocean Alley
Jolie and Scoobie High School Misadventures (prequel)
The Twain Does Meet (a Jolie and Scoobie novella)

River's Edge Mystery Series (Annie Acorn LLC Publishing)
From Newsprint to Footprints
Demise of a Devious Neighbor
Demise of a Devious Suspect

Logland Mystery Series
Tip a Hat to Murder
Final Cycle
Final Operation

http://www.elaineorr.com
http://elaineorr.blogspot.com

Whatever you do, enjoy reading!

The Twain Does Meet